"THE TURN OF THE SCREW

*. . . seems to have proved more fascinating to the
general reading public than anything else of James's
except DAISY MILLER . . ."* —Edmund Wilson

*In view of such a conclusion, it is fitting that these
two remarkable short novels should now be in-
cluded in a single volume. Both of them, one perhaps the most fascinating ghost story ever written,
the other a tragic drama of youth, have long been
considered among the most brilliant works of their
length ever written.*

DAISY MILLER, *once labeled "An outrage to American girlhood," deals with a theme to which James
devoted many of his longer novels, that of innocence brought to ruin, and is a classic of its kind.*

Of THE TURN OF THE SCREW, *noted critic Robert
Heilman has written:*
*"James has hit upon a fundamental truth of experi-
ence that no generation can ignore."*

Other titles by HENRY JAMES in LAUREL EDITIONS:

THE TURN OF
THE SCREW
and
DAISY MILLER

by Henry James

A LAUREL EDITION

Published by
DELL PUBLISHING CO., INC.
750 Third Avenue
New York, N.Y. 10017

Laurel ® TM 674623, Dell Publishing Co., Inc.

Reprinted by arrangement with
The Macmillan Company, New York, N.Y.

Cover painting by W. Brooks

First Dell printing—September, 1954
Second Dell printing—August, 1956
Third Dell printing—February, 1958
Fourth Dell printing—January, 1959
Fifth Dell printing—October, 1959
Sixth Dell printing—March, 1960
Seventh Dell printing—May, 1960
Eighth Dell printing—May, 1961
Ninth Dell printing—February, 1962
Tenth Dell printing—June, 1962
Eleventh Dell printing—December, 1962
Twelfth Dell printing—June, 1963
Thirteenth Dell printing—September, 1964
Fourteenth Dell printing—February, 1965
Fifteenth Dell printing—May, 1965
Sixteenth Dell printing—February, 1966
Seventeenth Dell printing—September, 1966
Eighteenth Dell printing—September, 1967
Nineteenth Dell printing—October, 1968
Twentieth Dell printing—September, 1969
Twenty-first Dell printing—December, 1969

Printed in U.S.A.

THE TURN
OF THE SCREW

The Turn of the Screw

THE STORY HAD HELD US, round the fire, sufficiently breathless, but except the obvious remark that it was gruesome, as, on Christmas eve in an old house, a strange tale should essentially be, I remember no comment uttered till somebody happened to say that it was the only case he had met in which such a visitation had fallen on a child. The case, I may mention, was that of an apparition in just such an old house as had gathered us for the occasion—an appearance, of a dreadful kind, to a little boy sleeping in the room with his mother and waking her up in the terror of it; waking her not to dissipate his dread and soothe him to sleep again, but to encounter also, herself, before she had succeeded in doing so, the same sight that had shaken him. It was this observation that drew from Douglas—not immediately, but later in the evening—a reply that had the interesting consequence to which I call attention. Someone else told a story not particularly effective, which I saw he was not following. This I took for a sign that he had himself something to produce and that we should only have to wait. We waited in fact till two nights later; but that same evening, before we scattered, he brought out what was in his mind.

"I quite agree—in regard to Griffin's ghost, or whatever it was—that its appearing first to the little boy, at so tender an age, adds a particular touch. But it's not the first occurrence of its charming kind that I know to have involved a child. If the child gives the effect another turn of the screw, what do you say to *two* children—?"

"We say, of course," somebody exclaimed, "that they give two turns! Also that we want to hear about them."

I can see Douglas there before the fire, to which he had got up to present his back, looking down at his interlocutor with his hands in his pockets. "Nobody but me, till

now, has ever heard. It's quite too horrible." This, natu
rally, was declared by several voices to give the thing th
utmost price, and our friend, with quiet art, prepared hi
triumph by turning his eyes over the rest of us and goin
on: "It's beyond everything. Nothing at all that I know
touches it."

"For sheer terror?" I remember asking.

He seemed to say it was not so simple as that; to b
really at a loss how to qualify it. He passed his hand ove
his eyes, made a little wincing grimace. "For dreadful-
dreadfulness!"

"Oh, how delicious!" cried one of the women.

He took no notice of her; he looked at me, but as if, in
stead of me, he saw what he spoke of. "For general un
canny ugliness and horror and pain."

"Well then," I said, "just sit right down and begin."

He turned round to the fire, gave a kick to a log, watche
it an instant. Then as he faced us again: "I can't begin
I shall have to send to town." There was a unanimou
groan at this, and much reproach; after which, in his pre
occupied way, he explained. "The story's written. It's in
locked drawer—it has not been out for years. I could writ
to my man and enclose the key; he could send down th
packet as he finds it." It was to me in particular that h
appeared to propound this—appeared almost to appeal fo
aid not to hesitate. He had broken a thickness of ice, th
formation of many a winter; had had his reasons for
long silence. The others resented postponement, but it wa
just his scruples that charmed me. I adjured him to writ
by the first post and to agree with us for an early hearing
then I asked him if the experience in question had beer
his own. To this his answer was prompt. "Oh, thank Goo
no!"

"And is the record yours? You took the thing down?"

"Nothing but the impression. I took that *here*"—h
tapped his heart. "I've never lost it."

"Then your manuscript—?"

"Is in old, faded ink, and in the most beautiful hand."

He hung fire again. "A woman's. She has been dead these twenty years. She sent me the pages in question before she died." They were all listening now, and of course there was somebody to be arch, or at any rate to draw the inference. But if he put the inference by without a smile it was also without irritation. "She was a most charming person, but she was ten years older than I. She was my sister's governess," he quietly said. "She was the most agreeable woman I've ever known in her position; she would have been worthy of any whatever. It was long ago, and this episode was long before. I was at Trinity, and I found her at home on my coming down the second summer. I was much there that year—it was a beautiful one; and we had, in her off-hours, some strolls and talks in the garden—talks in which she struck me as awfully clever and nice. Oh yes; don't grin: I liked her extremely and am glad to this day to think she liked me too. If she hadn't she wouldn't have told me. She had never told anyone. It wasn't simply that she said so, but that I knew she hadn't. I was sure; I could see. You'll easily judge why when you hear."

"Because the thing had been such a scare?"

He continued to fix me. "You'll easily judge," he repeated: "*you* will."

I fixed him too. "I see. She was in love."

He laughed for the first time. "You *are* acute. Yes, she was in love. That is, she had been. That came out—she couldn't tell her story without its coming out. I saw it, and she saw I saw it; but neither of us spoke of it. I remember the time and the place—the corner of the lawn, the shade of the great beeches and the long, hot summer afternoon. It wasn't a scene for a shudder; but oh—!" He quitted the fire and dropped back into his chair.

"You'll receive the packet Thursday morning?" I inquired.

"Probably not till the second post."

"Well then; after dinner—"

"You'll all meet me here?" He looked us round again.

"Isn't anybody going?" It was almost the tone of hop

"Everybody will stay!"

"*I* will—and *I* will!" cried the ladies whose departu had been fixed. Mrs. Griffin, however, expressed the ne for a little more light. "Who was it she was in love with

"The story will tell," I took upon myself to reply.

"Oh, I can't wait for the story!"

"The story *won't* tell," said Douglas; "not in any liter: vulgar way."

"More's the pity, then. That's the only way I ever u derstand."

"Won't *you* tell, Douglas?" somebody else inquired.

He sprang to his feet again. "Yes—tomorrow. Now must go to bed. Good-night." And quickly catching up candlestick, he left us slightly bewildered. From our e: of the great brown hall we heard his step on the sta: whereupon Mrs. Griffin spoke. "Well, if I don't know wl she was in love with, I know who *he* was."

"She was ten years older," said her husband.

"*Raison de plus*—at that age! But it's rather nice, l long reticence."

"Forty years!" Griffin put in.

"With this outbreak at last."

"The outbreak," I returned, "will make a tremendo occasion of Thursday night;" and everyone so agre with me that, in the light of it, we lost all attention f everything else. The last story, however incomplete a: like the mere opening of a serial, had been told; we ha: shook and "candlestuck," as somebody said, and went bed.

I knew the next day that a letter containing the k had, by the first post, gone off to his London apartmen but in spite of—or perhaps just on account of—the eve tual diffusion of this knowledge we quite let him alone t after dinner, till such an hour of the evening, in fact, might best accord with the kind of emotion on which o hopes were fixed. Then he became as communicative we could desire and indeed gave us his best reason for I ng so. We had it from him again before the fire in the all, as we had had our mild wonders of the previous ight. It appeared that the narrative he had promised to ead us really required for a proper intelligence a few vords of prologue. Let me say here distinctly, to have lone with it, that this narrative, from an exact transcript of my own made much later, is what I shall presently give. Poor Douglas, before his death—when it was in sight —committed to me the manuscript that reached him on he third of these days and that, on the same spot, with mmense effect, he began to read to our hushed little circle on the night of the fourth. The departing ladies who had said they would stay didn't, of course, thank heaven, tay: they departed, in consequence of arrangements made, n a rage of curiosity, as they professed, produced by the ouches with which he had already worked us up. But that only made his little final auditory more compact and elect, kept it, round the hearth, subject to a common hrill.

The first of these touches conveyed that the written tatement took up the tale at a point after it had, in a nanner, begun. The fact to be in possession of was therefore that his old friend, the youngest of several daughters of a poor country parson, had, at the age of twenty, on taking service for the first time in the schoolroom, come up to London, in trepidation, to answer in person an advertisement that had already placed her in brief correspondence with the advertiser. This person proved, on her presenting herself, for judgment, at a house in Harley Street, that impressed her as vast and imposing—this prospective patron proved a gentleman, a bachelor in the prime of life, such a figure as had never risen, save in a dream or an old novel, before a fluttered, anxious girl out of a Hampshire vicarage. One could easily fix his type; it never, happily, dies out. He was handsome and bold and pleasant, off-hand and gay and kind. He struck her, inevitably, as gallant and splendid, but what took her most of all and gave her the courage she afterwards

showed was that he put the whole thing to her as a kin
of favour, an obligation he should gratefully incur. Sh
conceived him as rich, but as fearfully extravagant—sa
him all in a glow of high fashion, of good looks, of exper
sive habits, of charming ways with women. He had fo
his own town residence a big house filled with the spoi
of travel and the trophies of the chase; but it was to h
country home, an old family place in Essex, that he wishe
her immediately to proceed.

He had been left, by the death of their parents in Indi
guardian to a small nephew and a small niece, childre
of a younger, a military brother, whom he had lost tw
years before. These children were, by the strangest c
chances for a man in his position,—a lone man withou
the right sort of experience or a grain of patience,—ver
heavily on his hands. It had all been a great worry an
on his own part doubtless, a series of blunders, but he in
mensely pitied the poor chicks and had done all he coul
had in particular sent them down to his other house, th
proper place for them being of course the country, an
kept them there, from the first, with the best people h
could find to look after them, parting even with his ow
servants to wait on them and going down himself, when
ever he might, to see how they were doing. The awkwar
thing was that they had practically no other relations an
that his own affairs took up all his time. He had put then
in possession of Bly, which was healthy and secure, an
had placed at the head of their little establishment—bu
below stairs only—an excellent woman, Mrs. Grose, whor
he was sure his visitor would like and who had formerl
been maid to his mother. She was now housekeeper an
was also acting for the time as superintendent to the littl
girl, of whom, without children of her own, she was, b
good luck, extremely fond. There were plenty of people t
help, but of course the young lady who should go down a
governess would be in supreme authority. She would als
have, in holidays, to look after the small boy, who had bee
for a term at school—young as he was to be sent, but wha

lse could be done?—and who, as the holidays were about
o begin, would be back from one day to the other. There
ad been for the two children at first a young lady whom
hey had had the misfortune to lose. She had done for
hem quite beautifully—she was a most respectable person
-till her death, the great awkwardness of which had, pre-
isely, left no alternative but the school for little Miles.
rs. Grose, since then, in the way of manners and things,
ad done as she could for Flora; and there were, further, a
ook, a housemaid, a dairywoman, an old pony, an old
room, and an old gardener, all likewise thoroughly re-
ectable.

So far had Douglas presented his picture when someone
ut a question. "And what did the former governess die
f?—of so much respectability?"

Our friend's answer was prompt. "That will come out.
don't anticipate."

"Excuse me—I thought that was just what you *are*
oing."

"In her successor's place," I suggested, "I should have
ished to learn if the office brought with it—"

"Necessary danger to life?" Douglas completed my
hought. "She did wish to learn, and she did learn. You
hall hear tomorrow what she learnt. Meanwhile, of
ourse, the prospect struck her as slightly grim. She was
oung, untried, nervous: it was a vision of serious duties
nd little company, of really great loneliness. She hesi-
ated—took a couple of days to consult and consider. But
he salary offered much exceeded her modest measure, and
n a second interview she faced the music, she engaged."
nd Douglas, with this, made a pause that, for the benefit
f the company, moved me to throw in—

"The moral of which was of course the seduction ex-
rcised by the splendid young man. She succumbed to it."

He got up and, as he had done the night before, went
o the fire, gave a stir to a log with his foot, then stood
moment with his back to us. "She saw him only twice."

"Yes, but that's just the beauty of her passion."

A little to my surprise, on this, Douglas turned rou~~nd~~ to me. "It *was* the beauty of it. There were others," ~~he~~ went on, "who hadn't succumbed. He told her frank~~ly~~ all his difficulty—that for several applicants the con~~di~~tions had been prohibitive. They were, somehow, simp~~ly~~ afraid. It sounded dull—it sounded strange; and all t~~he~~ more so because of his main condition."

"Which was—?"

"That she should never trouble him—but never, neve~~r~~ neither appeal nor complain nor write about anythi~~ng~~ only meet all questions herself, receive all moneys fr~~om~~ his solicitor, take the whole thing over and let him alo~~ne~~ She promised to do this, and she mentioned to me th~~at~~ when, for a moment, disburdened, delighted, he held h~~er~~ hand, thanking her for the sacrifice, she already felt ~~re~~warded."

"But was that all her reward?" one of the ladies aske~~d~~

"She never saw him again."

"Oh!" said the lady; which, as our friend immediat~~ely~~ left us again, was the only other word of importance c~~on~~tributed to the subject till, the next night, by the corn~~er~~ of the hearth, in the best chair, he opened the faded r~~ed~~ cover of a thin old-fashioned gilt-edged album. The wh~~ole~~ thing took indeed more nights than one, but on the fi~~rst~~ occasion the same lady put another question. "What ~~is~~ your title?"

"I haven't one."

"Oh, *I* have!" I said. But Douglas, without heeding m~~e~~ had begun to read with a fine clearness that was like~~ a~~ rendering to the ear of the beauty of his author's han~~d~~

1

I REMEMBER THE WHOLE BEGINNING as a succession of fligh~~ts~~ and drops, a little see-saw of the right throbs and t~~he~~ wrong. After rising, in town, to meet his appeal, I h~~ad~~

14

t all events a couple of very bad days—found myself doubtful again, felt indeed sure I had made a mistake. In his state of mind I spent the long hours of bumping, winging coach that carried me to the stopping-place at which I was to be met by a vehicle from the house. This convenience, I was told, had been ordered, and I found, toward the close of the June afternoon, a commodious fly in waiting for me. Driving at that hour, on a lovely day, through a country to which the summer sweetness seemed to offer me a friendly welcome, my fortitude mounted fresh and, as we turned into the avenue, encountered a reprieve that was probably but a proof of the point to which it had sunk. I suppose I had expected, or had dreaded, something so melancholy that what greeted me was a good surprise. I remember as a most pleasant impression the broad, clear front, its open windows and fresh curtains and the pair of maids looking out; I remember the lawn and the bright flowers and the crunch of my wheels on the gravel and the clustered treetops over which the rooks circled and cawed in the golden sky. The scene had a greatness that made it a different affair from my own scant home, and there immediately appeared at the door, with a little girl in her hand, a civil person who dropped me as decent a curtsey as if I had been the mistress or a distinguished visitor. I had received in Harley Street a narrower notion of the place, and that, as I recalled it, made me think the proprietor still more of a gentleman, suggested that what I was to enjoy might be something beyond his promise.

I had no drop again till the next day, for I was carried triumphantly through the following hours by my introduction to the younger of my pupils. The little girl who accompanied Mrs. Grose appeared to me on the spot a creature so charming as to make it a great fortune to have to do with her. She was the most beautiful child I had ever seen, and I afterwards wondered that my employer had not told me more of her. I slept little that night—I was too much excited; and this astonished me too, I recol-

lect, remained with me, adding to my sense of the libe
ality with which I was treated. The large, impressiv
room, one of the best in the house, the great state bed, a
I almost felt it, the full, figured draperies, the long glass
in which, for the first time, I could see myself from hea
to foot, all struck me—like the extraordinary charm o
my small charge—as so many things thrown in. It wa
thrown in as well, from the first moment, that I should ge
on with Mrs. Grose in a relation over which, on my way, i
the coach, I fear I had rather brooded. The only thin
indeed that in this early outlook might have made m
shrink again was the clear circumstance of her being s
glad to see me. I perceived within half an hour that sh
was so glad—stout, simple, plain, clean, wholesome woma
—as to be positively on her guard against showing it to
much. I wondered even then a little why she should wis
not to show it, and that, with reflection, with suspicio
might of course have made me uneasy.

But it was a comfort that there could be no uneasine
in a connection with anything so beatific as the radia
image of my little girl, the vision of whose angelic beaut
had probably more than anything else to do with th
restlessness that, before morning, made me several tim
rise and wander about my room to take in the whole pi
ture and prospect; to watch, from my open window, th
faint summer dawn, to look at such portions of the rest o
the house as I could catch, and to listen, while, in th
fading dusk, the first birds began to twitter, for the possibl
recurrence of a sound or two, less natural and not withou
but within, that I had fancied I heard. There had been
moment when I believed I recognised, faint and far, th
cry of a child; there had been another when I found my
self just consciously starting as at the passage, before m
door, of a light footstep. But these fancies were not marke
enough not to be thrown off, and it is only in the ligh
or the gloom, I should rather say, of other and subsequen
matters that they now come back to me. To watch, teac
"form" little Flora would too evidently be the making o

happy and useful life. It had been agreed between us
downstairs that after this first occasion I should have her
as a matter of course at night, her small white bed being
already arranged, to that end, in my room. What I had
undertaken was the whole care of her, and she had remained, just this last time, with Mrs. Grose only as an
effect of our consideration for my inevitable strangeness
and her natural timidity. In spite of this timidity—which
the child herself, in the oddest way in the world, had been
perfectly frank and brave about, allowing it, without a
sign of uncomfortable consciousness, with the deep, sweet
serenity indeed of one of Raphael's holy infants, to be discussed, to be imputed to her and to determine us—I felt
quite sure she would presently like me. It was part of what
I already liked Mrs. Grose herself for, the pleasure I could
see her feel in my admiration and wonder as I sat at supper
with four tall candles and with my pupil, in a high chair
and a bib, brightly facing me, between them, over bread
and milk. There were naturally things that in Flora's presence could pass between us only as prodigious and gratified looks, obscure and roundabout allusions.

"And the little boy—does he look like her? Is he too so
very remarkable?"

One wouldn't flatter a child. "Oh, Miss, *most* remarkable. If you think well of this one!"—and she stood there
with a plate in her hand, beaming at our companion, who
looked from one of us to the other with placid heavenly
eyes that contained nothing to check us.

"Yes; if I do—?"

"You *will* be carried away by the little gentleman!"

"Well, that, I think, is what I came for—to be carried
away. I'm afraid, however," I remember feeling the impulse to add, "I'm rather easily carried away. I was carried away in London!"

I can still see Mrs. Grose's broad face as she took this
in. "In Harley Street?"

"In Harley Street."

"Well, Miss, you're not the first—and you won't be the

17

last."

"Oh, I've no pretension," I could laugh, "to being t
only one. My other pupil, at any rate, as I understan
comes back tomorrow?"

"Not tomorrow—Friday, Miss. He arrives, as you di
by the coach, under care of the guard, and is to be m
by the same carriage."

I forthwith expressed that the proper as well as t
pleasant and friendly thing would be therefore that on t
arrival of the public conveyance I should be in waiti
for him with his little sister; an idea in which Mrs. Gro
concurred so heartily that I somehow took her manner
a kind of comforting pledge—never falsified, tha
heaven!—that we should on every question be quite at or
Oh, she was glad I was there!

What I felt the next day was, I suppose, nothing th
could be fairly called a reaction from the cheer of r
arrival; it was probably at the most only a slight oppr
sion produced by a fuller measure of the scale, as I walk
round them, gazed up at them, took them in, of my ne
circumstances. They had, as it were, an extent and ma
for which I had not been prepared and in the presen
of which I found myself, freshly, a little scared as well as
little proud. Lessons, in this agitation, certainly suffer
some delay; I reflected that my first duty was, by t
gentlest arts I could contrive, to win the child into t
sense of knowing me. I spent the day with her out
doors; I arranged with her, to her great satisfaction, th
it should be she, she only, who might show me the plac
She showed it step by step and room by room and secr
by secret, with droll, delightful, childish talk about
and with the result, in half an hour, of our becoming i
mense friends. Young as she was, I was struck, throug
out our little tour, with her confidence and courage wi
the way, in empty chambers and dull corridors, on crook
staircases that made me pause and even on the summit
an old machicolated square tower that made me dizzy, h
morning music, her disposition to tell me so many mo

things than she asked, rang out and led me on. I have not seen Bly since the day I left it, and I dare say that to my older and more informed eyes it would now appear sufficiently contracted. But as my little conductress, with her hair of gold and her frock of blue, danced before me round corners and pattered down passages, I had the view of a castle of romance inhabited by a rosy sprite, such a place as would somehow, for diversion of the young idea, take all colour out of storybooks and fairy-tales. Wasn't it just a storybook over which I had fallen a-doze and a-dream? No; it was a big, ugly, antique, but convenient house, embodying a few features of a building still older, half replaced and half utilised, in which I had the fancy of our being almost as lost as a handful of passengers in a great drifting ship. Well, I was, strangely, at the helm!

2

THIS CAME HOME TO ME when, two days later, I drove over with Flora to meet, as Mrs. Grose said, the little gentleman; and all the more for an incident that, presenting itself the second evening, had deeply disconcerted me. The first day had been, on the whole, as I have expressed, reassuring; but I was to see it wind up in keen apprehension. The postbag, that evening,—it came late,—contained a letter for me, which, however, in the hand of my employer, I found to be composed but of a few words enclosing another, addressed to himself, with a seal still unbroken. "This, I recognise, is from the head-master, and the head-master's an awful bore. Read him, please; deal with him; but mind you don't report. Not a word. I'm off!" I broke the seal with a great effort—so great a one that I was a long time coming to it; took the unopened missive at last up to my room and only attacked it just before going to bed. I had better have let it wait till morning, for it gave me a second sleepless night. With no coun-

sel to take, the next day, I was full of distress; and
finally got so the better of me that I determined to op·
myself at least to Mrs. Grose.

"What does it mean? The child's dismissed his school

She gave me a look that I remarked at the momer
then, visibly, with a quick blankness, seemed to try to ta
it back. "But aren't they all—?"

"Sent home—yes. But only for the holidays. Miles m
never go back at all."

Consciously, under my attention, she reddened. "Th
won't take him?"

"They absolutely decline."

At this she raised her eyes, which she had turned fro
me; I saw them fill with good tears. "What has he done

I hesitated; then I judged best simply to hand her m
letter—which, however, had the effect of making he
without taking it, simply put her hands behind her. Sh
shook her head sadly. "Such things are not for me, Miss

My counsellor couldn't read! I winced at my mistak
which I attenuated as I could, and opened my·letter aga
to repeat it to her; then, faltering in the act and foldir
it up once more, I put it back in my pocket. "Is he real
bad?"

The tears were still in her eyes. "Do the gentlemen s
so?"

"They go into no particulars. They simply express the
regret that it should be impossible to keep him. That c:
have only one meaning." Mrs. Grose listened with dun
emotion; she forebore to ask me what this meaning mig
be; so that, presently, to put the thing with some cohe
ence and with the mere aid of her presence to my ow
mind, I went on: "That he's an injury to the others."

At this, with one of the quick turns of simple folk, sh
suddenly flamed up. "Master Miles! *him* an injury?"

There was such a flood of good faith in it that, thoug
I had not yet seen the child, my very fears made me jun
to the absurdity of the idea. I found myself, to meet n
friend the better, offering it, on the spot, sarcastically. "T

is poor little innocent mates!"

"It's too dreadful," cried Mrs. Grose, "to say such cruel things! Why, he's scarce ten years old."

"Yes, yes; it would be incredible."

She was evidently grateful for such a profession. "See im, Miss, first. *Then* believe it!" I felt forthwith a new mpatience to see him; it was the beginning of a curiosity hat, for all the next hours, was to deepen almost to pain. Irs. Grose was aware, I could judge, of what she had pro-uced in me, and she followed it up with assurance. "You ight as well believe it of the little lady. Bless her," she dded the next moment—"*look* at her!"

I turned and saw that Flora, whom, ten minutes before, had established in the schoolroom with a sheet of white aper, a pencil, and a copy of nice "round O's," now pre-ented herself to view at the open door. She expressed in er little way an extraordinary detachment from disagree-ble duties, looking to me, however, with a great childish ght that seemed to offer it as a mere result of the affec-on she had conceived for my person, which had rendered ecessary that she should follow me. I needed nothing ore than this to feel the full force of Mrs. Grose's com-arison, and, catching my pupil in my arms, covered her ith kisses in which there was a sob of atonement.

None the less, the rest of the day, I watched for further ccasion to approach my colleague, especially as, toward vening, I began to fancy she rather sought to avoid me. overtook her, I remember, on the staircase; we went own together, and at the bottom I detained her, holding er there with a hand on her arm. "I take what you said o me at noon as a declaration that *you've* never known im to be bad."

She threw back her head; she had clearly, by this time, nd very honestly, adopted an attitude. "Oh, never known im—I don't pretend *that!*"

I was upset again. "Then you *have* known him—?"

"Yes indeed, Miss, thank God!"

On reflection I accepted this. "You mean that a boy

who never is—?"

"Is no boy for *me!*"

I held her tighter. "You like them with the spirit to [
naughty?" Then, keeping pace with her answer, "So (
I!" I eagerly brought out. "But not to the degree to co
taminate—"

"To contaminate?"—my big word left her at a loss.
explained it. "To corrupt."

She stared, taking my meaning in; but it produced
her an odd laugh. "Are you afraid he'll corrupt *you*
She put the question with such a fine bold humour th;
with a laugh, a little silly doubtless, to match her own,
gave way for the time to the apprehension of ridicule.

But the next day, as the hour for my drive approache
I cropped up in another place. "What was the lady wl
was here before?"

"The last governess? She was also young and pretty
almost as young and almost as pretty, Miss, even as you

"Ah, then, I hope her youth and her beauty help
her!" I recollect throwing off. "He seems to like us you
and pretty!"

"Oh, he *did*," Mrs. Grose assented: "it was the way l
liked everyone!" She had no sooner spoken indeed th;
she caught herself up. "I mean that's *his* way—the m;
ter's."

I was struck. "But of whom did you speak first?"

She looked blank, but she coloured. "Why, of *him*."

"Of the master?"

"Of who else?"

There was so obviously no one else that the next m
ment I had lost my impression of her having accidenta
said more than she meant; and I merely asked what
wanted to know. "Did *she* see anything in the boy—?"

"That wasn't right? She never told me."

I had a scruple, but I overcame it. "Was she carefu
particular?"

Mrs. Grose appeared to try to be conscientious. "Abo
some things—yes."

"But not about all?"

Again she considered. "Well, Miss—she's gone. I won't tell tales."

"I quite understand your feeling," I hastened to reply; but I thought it, after an instant, not opposed to this concession to pursue: "Did she die here?"

"No—she went off."

I don't know what there was in this brevity of Mrs. Grose's that struck me as ambiguous. "Went off to die?" Mrs. Grose looked straight out of the window, but I felt that, hypothetically, I had a right to know what young persons engaged for Bly were expected to do. "She was taken ill, you mean, and went home?"

"She was not taken ill, so far as appeared, in this house. She left it, at the end of the year, to go home, as she said, for a short holiday, to which the time she had put in had certainly given her a right. We had then a young woman—a nursemaid who had stayed on and who was a good girl and clever; and *she* took the children altogether for the interval. But our young lady never came back, and at the very moment I was expecting her I heard from the master that she was dead."

I turned this over. "But of what?"

"He never told me! But please, Miss," said Mrs. Grose, "I must get to my work."

3

HER THUS TURNING HER BACK ON ME was fortunately not, for my just preoccupations, a snub that could check the growth of our mutual esteem. We met, after I had brought home little Miles, more intimately than ever on the ground of my stupefaction, my general emotion: so monstrous was I then ready to pronounce it that such a child as had now been revealed to me should be under an interdict. I was a little late on the scene, and I felt, as he stood wist-

fully looking out for me before the door of the inn
which the coach had put him down, that I had seen hir
on the instant, without and within, in the great glow
freshness, the same positive fragrance of purity, in whic
I had, from the first moment, seen his little sister. He w
incredibly beautiful, and Mrs. Grose had put her finger c
it: everything but a sort of passion of tenderness for hi
was swept away by his presence. What I then and the
took him to my heart for was something divine that
have never found to the same degree in any child—his i
describable little air of knowing nothing in the world b
love. It would have been impossible to carry a bad nam
with a greater sweetness of innocence, and by the time
had got back to Bly with him I remained merely bew
dered—so far, that is, as I was not outraged—by the sen
of the horrible letter locked up in my room, in a drawe
As soon as I could compass a private word with Mrs. Gro
I declared to her that it was grotesque.

She promptly understood me. "You mean the cru
charge—?"

"It doesn't live an instant. My dear woman, *look*
him!"

She smiled at my pretension to have discovered h
charm. "I assure you, Miss, I do nothing else! What wi
you say, then?" she immediately added.

"In answer to the letter?" I had made up my min
"Nothing."

"And to his uncle?"

I was incisive. "Nothing."

"And to the boy himself?"

I was wonderful. "Nothing."

She gave with her apron a great wipe to her mout
"Then I'll stand by you. We'll see it out."

"We'll see it out!" I ardently echoed, giving her n
hand to make it a vow.

She held me there a moment, then whisked up her apro
again with her detached hand. "Would you mind, Miss,
I used the freedom—"

"To kiss me? No!" I took the good creature in my arms and, after we had embraced like sisters, felt still more mortified and indignant.

This, at all events, was for the time: a time so full that, as I recall the way it went, it reminds me of all the art I now need to make it a little distinct. What I look back at with amazement is the situation I accepted. I had undertaken, with my companion, to see it out, and I was under a charm, apparently, that could smooth away the extent and the far and difficult connections of such an effort. I was lifted aloft on a great wave of infatuation and pity. I found it simple, in my ignorance, my confusion, and perhaps my conceit, to assume that I could deal with a boy whose education for the world was all on the point of beginning. I am unable even to remember at this day what proposal I framed for the end of his holidays and the resumption of his studies. Lessons with me, indeed, that charming summer, we all had a theory that he was to have; but I now feel that, for weeks, the lessons must have been rather my own. I learnt something—at first certainly—that had not been one of the teachings of my small, smothered life; learnt to be amused, and even amusing, and not to think for the morrow. It was the first time, in a manner, that I had known space and air and freedom, all the music of summer and all the mystery of nature. And then there was consideration—and consideration was sweet. Oh, it was a trap—not designed, but deep—to my imagination, to my delicacy, perhaps to my vanity; to whatever, in me, was most excitable. The best way to picture it all is to say that I was off my guard. They gave me so little trouble—they were of a gentleness so extraordinary. I used to speculate—but even this with a dim disconnectedness—as to how the rough future (for all futures are rough!) would handle them and might bruise them. They had the bloom of health and happiness; and yet, as if I had been in charge of a pair of little grandees, of princes of the blood, for whom everything, to be right, would have to be enclosed and protected, the only form that, in my fancy, the after-

years could take for them was that of a romantic, a rea
royal extension of the garden and the park. It may be,
course, above all, that what suddenly broke into this gi
the previous time a charm of stillness—that hush in wh
something gathers or crouches. The change was actua
like the spring of a beast.

In the first weeks the days were long; they often,
their finest, gave me what I used to call my own hour,
hour when, for my pupils, tea-time and bed-time hav:
come and gone, I had, before my final retirement, a sm
interval alone. Much as I liked my companions, this ho
was the thing in the day I liked most; and I liked it b
of all when, as the light faded—or rather, I should say,
day lingered and the last calls of the last birds sound
in a flushed sky, from the old trees—I could take a tu
into the grounds and enjoy, almost with a sense of prope
that amused and flattered me, the beauty and dignity
the place. It was a pleasure at these moments to feel r
self tranquil and justified; doubtless, perhaps, also
reflect that by my discretion, my quiet good sense a
general high propriety, I was giving pleasure—if he e
thought of it!—to the person to whose pressure I had
sponded. What I was doing was what he had earnes
hoped and directly asked of me, and that I *could*, af
all, do it proved even a greater joy than I had expect
I dare say I fancied myself, in short, a remarkable you
woman and took comfort in the faith that this would m
publicly appear. Well, I needed to be remarkable to o:
a front to the remarkable things that presently gave th
first sign.

It was plump, one afternoon, in the middle of my v
hour: the children were tucked away and I had come
for my stroll. One of the thoughts that, as I don't in
least shrink now from noting, used to be with me in th
wanderings was that it would be as charming as a cha
ing story suddenly to meet someone. Someone would
pear there at the turn of a path and would stand bef
me and smile and approve. I didn't ask more than tha

I only asked that he should *know;* and the only way to be sure he knew would be to see it, and the kind light of it, in his handsome face. That was exactly present to me— by which I mean the face was—when, on the first of these occasions, at the end of a long June day, I stopped short on emerging from one of the plantations and coming into view of the house. What arrested me on the spot—and with a shock much greater than any vision had allowed for— was the sense that my imagination had, in a flash, turned real. He did stand there!—but high up, beyond the lawn and at the very top of the tower to which, on that first morning, little Flora had conducted me. This tower was one of a pair—square, incongruous, crenelated structures— that were distinguished, for some reason, though I could see little difference, as the new and the old. They flanked opposite ends of the house and were probably architectural absurdities, redeemed in a measure indeed by not being wholly disengaged nor of a height too pretentious, dating, in their gingerbread antiquity, from a romantic revival that was already a respectable past. I admired them, had fancies about them, for we could all profit in a degree, especially when they loomed through the dusk, by the grandeur of their actual battlements; yet it was not at such an elevation that the figure I had so often invoked seemed most in place.

It produced in me, this figure, in the clear twilight, I remember, two distinct gasps of emotion, which were, sharply, the shock of my first and that of my second surprise. My second was a violent perception of the mistake of my first: the man who met my eyes was not the person I had precipitately supposed. There came to me thus a bewilderment of vision of which, after these years, there is no living view that I can hope to give. An unknown man in a lonely place is a permitted object of fear to a young woman privately bred; and the figure that faced me was— a few more seconds assured me—as little anyone else I knew as it was the image that had been in my mind. I had not seen it in Harley Street—I had not seen it anywhere.

The place, moreover, in the strangest way in the worl
had, on the instant, and by the very fact of its appearanc
become a solitude. To me at least, making my statemer
here with a deliberation with which I have never made i
the whole feeling of the moment returns. It was as if, whi
I took in—what I did take in—all the rest of the scer
had been stricken with death. I can hear again, as I writ
the intense hush in which the sounds of evening droppe
The rooks stopped cawing in the golden sky and th
friendly hour lost, for the minute, all its voice. But ther
was no other change in nature, unless indeed it were
change that I saw with a stranger sharpness. The gold wa
still in the sky, the clearness in the air, and the man wh
looked at me over the battlements was as definite as
picture in a frame. That's how I thought, with extraord
nary quickness, of each person that he might have bee
and that he was not. We were confronted across our di
tance quite long enough for me to ask myself with inter
sity who then he was and to feel, as an effect of my inabili
to say, a wonder that in a few instants more became intens

The great question, or one of these, is, afterwards,
know, with regard to certain matters, the question o
how long they have lasted. Well, this matter of min
think what you will of it, lasted while I caught at a doze
possibilities, none of which made a difference for th
better, that I could see, in there having been in the house
and for how long, above all?—a person of whom I was i
ignorance. It lasted while I just bridled a little with th
sense that my office demanded that there should be n
such ignorance and no such person. It lasted while th
visitant, at all events,—and there was a touch of the strang
freedom, as I remember, in the sign of familiarity of h
wearing no hat,—seemed to fix me, from his position, wit
just the question, just the scrutiny through the fadin
light, that his own presence provoked. We were too fa
apart to call to each other, but there was a moment a
which, at shorter range, some challenge between us, breal
ing the hush, would have been the right result of ou

straight mutual stare. He was in one of the angles, the one away from the house, very erect, as it struck me, and with both hands on the ledge. So I saw him as I see the letters I form on this page; then, exactly, after a minute, as if to add to the spectacle, he slowly changed his place—passed, looking at me hard all the while, to the opposite corner of the platform. Yes, I had the sharpest sense that during this transit he never took his eyes from me, and I can see at this moment the way his hand, as he went, passed from one of the crenelations to the next. He stopped at the other corner, but less long, and even as he turned away still markedly fixed me. He turned away; that was all I knew.

4

IT WAS NOT THAT I DIDN'T WAIT, on this occasion, for more, for I was rooted as deeply as I was shaken. Was there a "secret" at Bly—a mystery of Udolpho or an insane, an unmentionable relative kept in unsuspected confinement? I can't say how long I turned it over, or how long, in a confusion of curiosity and dread, I remained where I had my collision; I only recall that when I re-entered the house darkness had quite closed in. Agitation, in the interval, certainly had held me and driven me, for I must, in circling about the place, have walked three miles; but I was to be, later on, so much more overwhelmed that this mere dawn of alarm was a comparatively human chill. The most singular part of it in fact—singular as the rest had been—was the part I became, in the hall, aware of in meeting Mrs. Grose. This picture comes back to me in the general train—the impression, as I received it on my return, of the wide white panelled space, bright in the lamplight and with its portraits and red carpet, and of the good surprised look of my friend, which immediately told me she had missed me. It came to me straightway, under

her contact, that, with plain heartiness, mere relieve
anxiety at my appearance, she knew nothing whateve
that could bear upon the incident I had there ready fo
her. I had not suspected in advance that her comfortab!
face would pull me up, and I somehow measured the im
portance of what I had seen by my thus finding myse
hesitate to mention it. Scarce anything in the whole histor
seems to me so odd as this fact that my real beginning o
fear was one, as I may say, with the instinct of sparin
my companion. On the spot, accordingly, in the pleasar
hall and with her eyes on me, I, for a reason that I couldn
then have phrased, achieved an inward revolution—offere
a vague pretext for my lateness and, with the plea of th
beauty of the night and of the heavy dew and wet fee
went as soon as possible to my room.

Here it was another affair; here, for many days afte
it was a queer affair enough. There were hours, from da
to day,—or at least there were moments, snatched eve
from clear duties,—when I had to shut myself up to thin!
It was not so much yet that I was more nervous than
could bear to be as that I was remarkably afraid of be
coming so; for the truth I had now to turn over wa
simply and clearly, the truth that I could arrive at n
account whatever of the visitor with whom I had been s
inexplicably and yet, as it seemed to me, so intimatel
concerned. It took little time to see that I could soun
without forms of inquiry and without exciting remar
any domestic complication. The shock I had suffere
must have sharpened all my senses; I felt sure, at the en
of three days and as the result of mere closer attention
that I had not been practised upon by the servants no
made the object of any "game." Of whatever it was tha
I knew nothing was known around me. There was bu
one sane inference: someone had taken a liberty rathe
gross. That was what, repeatedly, I dipped into my roor
and locked the door to say to myself. We had been, collec
tively, subject to an intrusion; some unscrupulous trave
ler, curious in old houses, had made his way in unobserved

30

njoyed the prospect from the best point of view, and
hen stolen out as he came. If he had given me such a
old hard stare, that was but a part of his indiscretion.
The good thing, after all, was that we should surely see no
nore of him.

This was not so good a thing, I admit, as not to leave
ne to judge that what, essentially, made nothing else
nuch signify was simply my charming work. My charm-
ng work was just my life with Miles and Flora, and
hrough nothing could I so like it as through feeling that
I could throw myself into it in trouble. The attraction of
ny small charges was a constant joy, leading me to wonder
afresh at the vanity of my original fears, the distaste I had
begun by entertaining for the probable grey prose of my
office. There was to be no grey prose, it appeared, and no
long grind; so how could work not be charming that presented itself as daily beauty? It was all the romance of
the nursery and the poetry of the schoolroom. I don't mean
by this, of course, that we studied only fiction and verse; I
mean I can express no otherwise the sort of interest my
companions inspired. How can I describe that except by
saying that instead of growing used to them—and it's a
marvel for a governess: I call the sisterhood to witness!—
I made constant fresh discoveries. There was one direction, assuredly, in which these discoveries stopped: deep
obscurity continued to cover the region of the boy's con-
duct at school. It had been promptly given me, I have
noted, to face that mystery without a pang. Perhaps even
it would be nearer the truth to say that—without a word—
he himself had cleared it up. He had made the whole
charge absurd. My conclusion bloomed there with the
real rose-flush of his innocence: he was only too fine and
fair for the little horrid, unclean school-world, and he had
paid a price for it. I reflected acutely that the sense of such
differences, such superiorities of quality, always, on the
part of the majority—which could include even stupid,
sordid head-masters—turns infallibly to the vindictive.

Both the children had a gentleness (it was their only

fault, and it never made Miles a muff) that kept them
how shall I express it?—almost impersonal and certain
quite unpunishable. They were like the cherubs of th
anecdote, who had—morally, at any rate—nothing
whack! I remember feeling with Miles in especial as if h
had had, as it were, no history. We expect of a small chil
a scant one, but there was in this beautiful little bo
something extraordinarily sensitive, yet extraordinari
happy, that, more than in any creature of his age I hav
seen, struck me as beginning anew each day. He had neve
for a second suffered. I took this as a direct disproof of h
having really been chastised. If he had been wicked h
would have "caught" it, and I should have caught it b
the rebound—I should have found the trace. I found not
ing at all, and he was therefore angel. He never spoke o
his school, never mentioned a comrade or a master; and
for my part, was quite too much disgusted to allude t
them. Of course I was under the spell, and the wonderfu
part is that, even at the time, I perfectly knew I was. Bu
I gave myself up to it; it was an antidote to any pain, an
I had more pains than one. I was in receipt in these day
of disturbing letters from home, where things were no
going well. But with my children, what things in th
world mattered? That was the question I used to put t
my scrappy retirements. I was dazzled by their lovelines

There was a Sunday—to get on—when it rained wit
such force and for so many hours that there could be n
procession to church; in consequence of which, as the da
declined, I had arranged with Mrs. Grose that, shoul
the evening show improvement, we would attend togethe
the late service. The rain happily stopped, and I prepare
for our walk, which, through the park and by the goo
road to the village, would be a matter of twenty minute
Coming downstairs to meet my colleague in the hall, I re
membered a pair of gloves that had required three stitche
and that had received them—with a publicity perhaps no
edifying—while I sat with the children at their tea, serve
on Sundays, by exception, in that cold, clean temple o

ahogany and brass, the "grown-up" dining-room. The
oves had been dropped there, and I turned in to recover
em. The day was grey enough, but the afternoon light
ll lingered, and it enabled me, on crossing the threshold,
ot only to recognise, on a chair near the wide window,
en closed, the articles I wanted, but to become aware of
person on the other side of the window and looking
raight in. One step into the room had sufficed; my vision
as instantaneous; it was all there. The person looking
raight in was the person who had already appeared to
e. He appeared thus again with I won't say greater
stinctness, for that was impossible, but with a nearness
at represented a forward stride in our intercourse and
ade me, as I met him, catch my breath and turn cold. He
as the same—he was the same, and seen, this time, as he
d been seen before, from the waist up, the window,
ough the dining-room was on the ground-floor, not
ing down to the terrace on which he stood. His face
as close to the glass, yet the effect of this better view
as, strangely, only to show me how intense the former
d been. He remained but a few seconds—long enough
convince me he also saw and recognised; but it was
if I had been looking at him for years and had known
m always. Something, however, happened this time
at had not happened before; his stare into my face,
rough the glass and across the room, was as deep and
rd as then, but it quitted me for a moment during which
could still watch it, see it fix successively several other
ings. On the spot there came to me the added shock of a
rtitude that it was not for me he had come there. He had
me for someone else.

The flash of this knowledge—for it was knowledge in the
dst of dread—produced in me the most extraordinary
ect, started, as I stood there, a sudden vibration of duty
d courage. I say courage because I was beyond all doubt
eady far gone. I bounded straight out of the door again,
ached that of the house, got, in an instant, upon the
ive, and, passing along the terrace as fast as I could

rush, turned a corner and came full in sight. But it was
sight of nothing now—my visitor had vanished. I stopp
I almost dropped, with the real relief of this; but I took
the whole scene—I gave him time to reappear. I c
it time, but how long was it? I can't speak to the purp
today of the duration of these things. That kind
measure must have left me: they couldn't have lasted
they actually appeared to me to last. The terrace and t
whole place, the lawn and the garden beyond it, all
could see of the park, were empty with a great emptine
There were shrubberies and big trees, but I remember t
clear assurance I felt that none of them concealed him. I
was there or was not there: not there if I didn't see him
got hold of this; then, instinctively, instead of returning
I had come, went to the window. It was confusedly pr
ent to me that I ought to place myself where he had stoc
I did so; I applied my face to the pane and looked, as
had looked, into the room. As if, at this moment, to sho
me exactly what his range had been, Mrs. Grose, as I h
done for himself just before, came in from the hall. Wi
this I had the full image of a repetition of what h
already occurred. She saw me as I had seen my own vis
ant; she pulled up short as I had done; I gave her som
thing of the shock that I had received. She turned whi
and this made me ask myself if I had blanched as mud
She stared, in short, and retreated on just *my* lines, and
knew she had then passed out and come round to me a
that I should presently meet her. I remained where I w
and while I waited I thought of more things than on
But there's only one I take space to mention. I wonder
why *she* should be scared.

5

OH, SHE LET ME KNOW as soon as, round the corner of t
house, she loomed again into view. "What in the name

oodness is the matter—?" She was now flushed and out
f breath.

I said nothing till she came quite near. "With me?" I
ust have made a wonderful face. "Do I show it?"

"You're as white as a sheet. You look awful."

I considered; I could meet on this, without scruple, any
nocence. My need to respect the bloom of Mrs. Grose's
ad dropped, without a rustle, from my shoulders, and if
wavered for the instant it was not with what I kept back.
put out my hand to her and she took it; I held her hard
little, liking to feel her close to me. There was a kind of
pport in the shy heave of her surprise. "You came for
e for church, of course, but I can't go."

"Has anything happened?"

"Yes. You must know now. Did I look very queer?"

"Through this window? Dreadful!"

"Well," I said, "I've been frightened." Mrs. Grose's eyes
xpressed plainly that *she* had no wish to be, yet also that
e knew too well her place not to be ready to share with
e any marked inconvenience. Oh, it was quite settled
at she *must* share! "Just what you saw from the dining-
oom a minute ago was the effect of that. What *I* saw—
st before—was much worse."

Her hand tightened. "What was it?"

"An extraordinary man. Looking in."

"What extraordinary man?" ·

"I haven't the least idea."

Mrs. Grose gazed round us in vain. "Then where is he
ne?"

"I know still less."

"Have you seen him before?"

"Yes—once. On the old tower."

She could only look at me harder. "Do you mean he's a
ranger?"

"Oh, very much!"

"Yet you didn't tell me?"

"No—for reasons. But now that you've guessed—"

Mrs. Grose's round eyes encountered this charge. "Ah,

I haven't guessed!" she said very simply. "How can I
you don't imagine?"

"I don't in the very least."

"You've seen him nowhere but on the tower?"

"And on this spot just now."

Mrs. Grose looked round again. "What was he doing (
the tower?"

"Only standing there and looking down at me."

She thought a minute. "Was he a gentleman?"

I found I had no need to think. "No." She gazed
deeper wonder. "No."

"Then nobody about the place? Nobody from tl
village?"

"Nobody—nobody. I didn't tell you, but I made sure

She breathed a vague relief: this was, oddly, so much
the good. It only went indeed a little way. "But if he isr
a gentleman—"

"What *is* he? He's a horror."

"A horror?"

"He's—God help me if I know *what* he is!"

Mrs. Grose looked round once more; she fixed her ey
on the duskier distance, then, pulling herself togethe
turned to me with abrupt inconsequence. "It's time v
should be at church."

"Oh, I'm not fit for church!"

"Won't it do you good?"

"It won't do *them*—!" I nodded at the house.

"The children?"

"I can't leave them now."

"You're afraid—?"

I spoke boldly. "I'm afraid of *him*."

Mrs. Grose's large face showed me, at this, for the fir
time, the far-away faint glimmer of a consciousness mo
acute: I somehow made out in it the delayed dawn of a
idea I myself had not given her and that was as yet qui
obscure to me. It comes back to me that I thought i
stantly of this as something I could get from her; and
felt it to be connected with the desire she presently showe

know more. "When was it—on the tower?"

"About the middle of the month. At this same hour."

"Almost at dark?" said Mrs. Grose.

"Oh, no, not nearly. I saw him as I see you."

"Then how did he get in?"

"And how did he get out?" I laughed. "I had no oppor-
nity to ask him! This evening, you see," I pursued, "he
s not been able to get in."

"He only peeps?"

"I hope it will be confined to that!" She had now let
my hand; she turned away a little. I waited an instant;
en I brought out: "Go to church. Good-bye. I must
tch."

Slowly she faced me again. "Do you fear for them?"

We met in another long look. "Don't *you?*" Instead of
swering she came nearer to the window and, for a min-
e, applied her face to the glass. "You see how he could
," I meanwhile went on.

She didn't move. "How long was he here?"

"Till I came out. I came to meet him."

Mrs. Grose at last turned round, and there was still
re in her face. "*I* couldn't have come out."

"Neither could I!" I laughed again. "But I did come.
ave my duty."

"So have I mine," she replied; after which she added:
/hat is he like?"

"I've been dying to tell you. But he's like nobody."

"Nobody?" she echoed.

"He has no hat." Then seeing in her face that she
eady, in this, with a deeper dismay, found a touch of
:ture, I quickly added stroke to stroke. "He has red hair,
y red, close-curling, and a pale face, long in shape, with
aight, good features and little, rather queer whiskers
at are as red as his hair. His eyebrows are, somehow,
rker; they look particularly arched and as if they might
>ve a good deal. His eyes are sharp, strange—awfully;
t I only know clearly that they're rather small and very
ed. His mouth's wide, and his lips are thin, and except

37

for his little whiskers he's quite clean-shaven. He gives
a sort of sense of looking like an actor."

"An actor!" It was impossible to resemble one less,
least, than Mrs. Grose at that moment.

"I've never seen one, but so I suppose them. He's t
active, erect," I continued, "but never—no, never!—a g
tleman."

My companion's face had blanched as I went on;
round eyes started and her mild mouth gaped. "A gen
man?" she gasped, confounded, stupefied: "a gentlen
he?"

"You know him then?"

She visibly tried to hold herself. "But he *is* handsom

I saw the way to help her. "Remarkably!"

"And dressed—?"

"In somebody's clothes. They're smart, but they're
his own."

She broke into a breathless affirmative groan. "They
the master's!"

I caught it up. "You *do* know him?"

She faltered but a second. "Quint!" she cried.

"Quint?"

"Peter Quint—his own man, his valet, when he
here!"

"When the master was?"

Gaping still, but meeting me, she pieced it all togeth
"He never wore his hat, but he did wear—well, there w
waistcoats missed! They were both here—last year. Th
the master went, and Quint was alone."

I followed, but halting a little. "Alone?"

"Alone with *us*." Then, as from a deeper depth, "
charge," she added.

"And what became of him?"

She hung fire so long that I was still more mystifi
"He went too," she brought out at last.

"Went where?"

Her expression, at this, became extraordinary. "G
knows where! He died."

"Died?" I almost shrieked.

She seemed fairly to square herself, plant herself more firmly to utter the wonder of it. "Yes. Mr. Quint is dead."

6

IT TOOK OF COURSE more than that particular passage to place us together in presence of what we had now to live with as we could—my dreadful liability to impressions of the order so vividly exemplified, and my companion's knowledge, henceforth,—a knowledge half consternation and half compassion,—of that liability. There had been, this evening, after the revelation that left me, for an hour, so prostrate—there had been, for either of us, no attendance on any service but a little service of tears and vows, of prayers and promises, a climax to the series of mutual challenges and pledges that had straightway ensued on our retreating together to the schoolroom and shutting ourselves up there to have everything out. The result of our having everything out was simply to reduce our situation to the last rigour of its elements. She herself had seen nothing, not the shadow of a shadow, and nobody in the house but the governess was in the governess's plight; yet she accepted without directly impugning my sanity the truth as I gave it to her, and ended by showing me, on this ground, an awe-stricken tenderness, an expression of the sense of my more than questionable privilege, of which the very breath has remained with me as that of the sweetest of human charities.

What was settled between us, accordingly, that night, was that we thought we might bear things together; and I was not even sure that, in spite of her exemption, it was she who had the best of the burden. I knew at this hour, I think, as well as I knew later what I was capable of meeting to shelter my pupils; but it took me some time to be wholly sure of what my honest ally was prepared for to

keep terms with so compromising a contract. I was quee
company enough—quite as queer as the company I re
ceived; but as I trace over what we went through I se
how much common ground we must have found in th
one idea that, by good fortune, *could* steady us. It was th
idea, the second movement, that led me straight out, as
may say, of the inner chamber of my dread. I could tak
the air in the court, at least, and there Mrs. Grose coul
join me. Perfectly can I recall now the particular wa
strength came to me before we separated for the night. W
had gone over and over every feature of what I had seen

"He was looking for someone else, you say—someon
who was not you?"

"He was looking for little Miles." A portentous clear
ness now possessed me. *"That's* whom he was looking for."

"But how do you know?"

"I know, I know, I know!" My exaltation grew. "An
you know, my dear!"

She didn't deny this, but I required, I felt, not even s
much telling as that. She resumed in a moment, at an'
rate: "What if *he* should see him?"

"Little Miles? That's what he wants!"

She looked immensely scared again. "The child?"

"Heaven forbid! The man. He wants to appear t
them." That he might was an awful conception, and yet
somehow, I could keep it at bay; which, moreover, as w
lingered there, was what I succeeded in practically prov
ing. I had an absolute certainty that I could see again wha
I had already seen, but something within me said tha
by offering myself bravely as the sole subject of such ex
perience, by accepting, by inviting, by surmounting it all
I should serve as an expiatory victim and guard the tran
quillity of my companions. The children, in especial,
should thus fence about and absolutely save. I recall on
of the last things I said that night to Mrs. Grose.

"It does strike me that my pupils have never men
tioned—"

She looked at me hard as I musingly pulled up. "Hi

aving been here and the time they were with him?"

"The time they were with him, and his name, his presnce, his history, in any way."

"Oh, the little lady doesn't remember. She never heard r knew."

"The circumstances of his death?" I thought with some ntensity. "Perhaps not. But Miles would remember—Iiles would know."

"Ah, don't try him!" broke from Mrs. Grose.

I returned her the look she had given me. "Don't be fraid." I continued to think. "It *is* rather odd."

"That he has never spoken of him?"

"Never by the least allusion. And you tell me they were great friends'?"

"Oh, it wasn't *him!*" Mrs. Grose with emphasis declared. It was Quint's own fancy. To play with him, I mean—to poil him." She paused a moment; then she added: "Quint as much too free."

This gave me, straight from my vision of his face—*such* face—a sudden sickness of disgust. "Too free with *my* oy?"

"Too free with everyone!"

I forebore, for the moment, to analyse this description urther than by the reflection that a part of it applied to everal of the members of the household, or the half-dozen naids and men who were still of our small colony. But here was everything, for our apprehension, in the lucky act that no discomfortable legend, no perturbation of cullions, had ever, within anyone's memory, attached to he kind old place. It had neither bad name nor ill fame, nd Mrs. Grose, most apparently, only desired to cling to ne and to quake in silence. I even put her, the very last hing of all, to the test. It was when, at midnight, she had er hand on the schoolroom door to take leave. "I have it rom you then—for it's of great importance—that he was efinitely and admittedly bad?"

"Oh, not admittedly. *I* knew it—but the master didn't."

"And you never told him?"

"Well, he didn't like tale-bearing—he hated complain[
He was terribly short with anything of that kind, and
people were all right to *him*—"

"He wouldn't be bothered with more?" This squar[
well enough with my impression of him: he was not
trouble-loving gentleman, nor so very particular perha[
about some of the company *he* kept. All the same, I press[
my interlocutress. "I promise you *I* would have told!"

She felt my discrimination. "I dare say I was wron[
But, really, I was afraid."

"Afraid of what?"

"Of things that man could do. Quint was so clever—[
was so deep."

I took this in still more than, probably, I showed. "Y[
weren't afraid of anything else? Not of his effect—?"

"His effect?" she repeated with a face of anguish an[
waiting while I faltered.

"On innocent little precious lives. They were in yo[
charge."

"No, they were not in mine!" she roundly and distres[
fully returned. "The master believed in him and place[
him here because he was supposed not to be well and th[
country air so good for him. So he had everything to sa[
Yes"—she let me have it—"even about *them.*"

"Them—that creature?" I had to smother a kind [
howl. "And you could bear it!"

"No, I couldn't—and I can't now!" And the poor woma[
burst into tears.

A rigid control, from the next day, was, as I have sai[
to follow them; yet how often and how passionately, f[
a week, we came back together to the subject! Much [
we had discussed it that Sunday night, I was, in the in[
mediate later hours in especial—for it may be imagine[
whether I slept—still haunted with the shadow of som[
thing she had not told me. I myself had kept back not[
ing, but there was a word Mrs. Grose had kept back. I w[
sure, moreover, by morning, that this was not from a fai[
ure of frankness, but because on every side there we[

fears. It seems to me indeed, in retrospect, that by the time the morrow's sun was high I had restlessly read into the facts before us almost all the meaning they were to receive from subsequent and more cruel occurrences. What they gave me above all was just the sinister figure of the living man—the dead one would keep awhile!—and of the months he had continuously passed at Bly, which, added up, made a formidable stretch. The limit of this evil time had arrived only when, on the dawn of a winter's morning, Peter Quint was found, by a labourer going to early work, stone dead on the road from the village: a catastrophe explained—superficially at least—by a visible wound to his head; such a wound as might have been produced—and as, on the final evidence, *had* been—by a fatal slip, in the dark and after leaving the public house, on the steepish icy slope, a wrong path, altogether, at the bottom of which he lay. The icy slope, the turn mistaken at night and in liquor, accounted for much—practically, in the end and after the inquest and boundless chatter, for everything; but there had been matters in his life —strange passages and perils, secret disorders, vices more than suspected—that would have accounted for a good deal more.

I scarce know how to put my story into words that shall be a credible picture of my state of mind; but I was in these days literally able to find a joy in the extraordinary flight of heroism the occasion demanded of me. I now saw that I had been asked for a service admirable and difficult; and there would be a greatness in letting it be seen—oh, in the right quarter!—that I could succeed where many another girl might have failed. It was an immense help to me—I confess I rather applaud myself as I look back!—that I saw my service so strongly and so simply. I was there to protect and defend the little creatures in the world the most bereaved and the most loveable, the appeal of whose helplessness had suddenly become only too explicit, a deep, constant ache of one's own committed heart. We were cut off, really, together; we

were united in our danger. They had nothing but me, and
I—well, I had *them*. It was in short a magnificent chance
This chance presented itself to me in an image richly
material. I was a screen—I was to stand before them. The
more I saw, the less they would. I began to watch them in
a stifled suspense, a disguised excitement that might well
had it continued too long, have turned to something like
madness. What saved me, as I now see, was that it turned
to something else altogether. It didn't last as suspense—it
was superseded by horrible proofs. Proofs, I say, yes—from
the moment I really took hold.

This moment dated from an afternoon hour that I happened to spend in the grounds with the younger of my
pupils alone. We had left Miles indoors, on the red cushion
of a deep window-seat; he had wished to finish a book, and
I had been glad to encourage a purpose so laudable in a
young man whose only defect was an occasional excess of
the restless. His sister, on the contrary, had been alert to
come out, and I strolled with her half an hour, seeking
the shade, for the sun was still high and the day exception-
ally warm. I was aware afresh, with her, as we went, of
how, like her brother, she contrived—it was the charming
thing in both children—to let me alone without appearing
to drop me and to accompany me without appearing to
surround. They were never importunate and yet never
listless. My attention to them all really went to seeing
them amuse themselves immensely without me: this was
a spectacle they seemed actively to prepare and that engaged me as an active admirer. I walked in a world of their
invention—they had no occasion whatever to draw upon
mine; so that my time was taken only with being, for
them, some remarkable person or thing that the game of
the moment required and that was merely, thanks to my
superior, my exalted stamp, a happy and highly distinguished sinecure. I forget what I was on the present occasion; I only remember that I was something very
important and very quiet and that Flora was playing very
hard. We were on the edge of the lake, and, as we had

ately begun geography, the lake was the Sea of Azof.

Suddenly, in these circumstances, I became aware that, on the other side of the Sea of Azof, we had an interested spectator. The way this knowledge gathered in me was the strangest thing in the world—the strangest, that is, except the very much stranger in which it quickly merged itself. I had sat down with a piece of work—for I was something or other that could sit—on the old stone bench which overlooked the pond; and in this position I began to take in with certitude, and yet without direct vision, the presence, at a distance, of a third person. The old trees, the thick shrubbery, made a great and pleasant shade, but it was all suffused with the brightness of the hot, still hour. There was no ambiguity in anything; none whatever, at least, in the conviction I from one moment to another found myself forming as to what I should see straight before me and across the lake as a consequence of raising my eyes. They were attached at this juncture to the stitching in which I was engaged, and I can feel once more the spasm of my effort not to move them till I should so have steadied myself as to be able to make up my mind what to do. There was an alien object in view—a figure whose right of presence I instantly, passionately questioned. I recollect counting over perfectly the possibilities, reminding myself that nothing was more natural, for instance, than the appearance of one of the men about the place, or even of a messenger, a postman or a tradesman's boy, from the village. That reminder had as little effect on my practical certitude as I was conscious—still even without looking—of its having upon the character and attitude of our visitor. Nothing was more natural than that these things should be the other things that they absolutely were not.

Of the positive identity of the apparition I would assure myself as soon as the small clock of my courage should have ticked out the right second; meanwhile, with an effort that was already sharp enough, I transferred my eyes straight to little Flora, who, at the moment, was about ten yards away. My heart had stood still for an

instant with the wonder and terror of the question whethe
she too would see; and I held my breath while I waited fo
what a cry from her, what some sudden innocent sig
either of interest or of alarm, would tell me. I waited, bu
nothing came; then, in the first place—and there is some
thing more dire in this, I feel, than in anything I hav
to relate—I was determined by a sense that, within a min
ute, all sounds from her had previously dropped; and, i
the second, by the circumstance that, also within the min
ute, she had, in her play, turned her back to the water
This was her attitude when I at last looked at her—looke
with the confirmed conviction that we were still, together
under direct personal notice. She had picked up a smal
flat piece of wood, which happened to have in it a littl
hole that had evidently suggested to her the idea of stick
ing in another fragment that might figure as a mast an
make the thing a boat. This second morsel, as I watche
her, she was very markedly and intently attempting t
tighten in its place. My apprehension of what she wa
doing sustained me so that after some seconds I felt I wa
ready for more. Then I again shifted my eyes—I faced wha
I had to face.

7

I GOT HOLD OF MRS. GROSE as soon after this as I could
and I can give no intelligible account of how I fought ou
the interval. Yet I still hear myself cry as I fairly thre
myself into her arms: "They *know*—it's too monstrous
they know, they know!"

"And what on earth—?" I felt her incredulity as sh
held me.

"Why, all that *we* know—and heaven knows what els
besides!" Then, as she released me, I made it out to he
made it out perhaps only now with full coherency even t
myself. "Two hours ago, in the garden"—I could scarc

articulate—"Flora *saw!*"

Mrs. Grose took it as she might have taken a blow in the stomach. "She has told you?" she panted.

"Not a word—that's the horror. She kept it to herself! The child of eight, *that* child!" Unutterable still, for me, was the stupefaction of it.

Mrs. Grose, of course, could only gape the wider. "Then how do you know?"

"I was there—I saw with my eyes: saw that she was perfectly aware."

"Do you mean aware of *him?*"

"No—of *her.*" I was conscious as I spoke that I looked prodigious things, for I got the slow reflection of them in my companion's face. "Another person—this time; but a figure of quite as unmistakeable horror and evil: a woman in black, pale and dreadful—with such an air also, and such a face!—on the other side of the lake. I was there with the child—quiet for the hour; and in the midst of it she came."

"Came how—from where?"

"From where they come from! She just appeared and stood there—but not so near."

"And without coming nearer?"

"Oh, for the effect and the feeling, she might have been as close as you!"

My friend, with an odd impulse, fell back a step. "Was she someone you've never seen?"

"Yes. But someone the child has. Someone *you* have." Then, to show how I had thought it all out: "My predecessor—the one who died."

"Miss Jessel?"

"Miss Jessel. You don't believe me?" I pressed.

She turned right and left in her distress. "How can you be sure?"

This drew from me, in the state of my nerves, a flash of impatience. "Then ask Flora—*she's* sure!" But I had no sooner spoken than I caught myself up. "No, for God's sake, *don't!* She'll say she isn't—she'll lie!"

Mrs. Grose was not too bewildered instinctively to protest. "Ah, how *can* you?"

"Because I'm clear. Flora doesn't want me to know."

"It's only then to spare you."

"No, no—there are depths, depths! The more I go over it, the more I see in it, and the more I see in it the more I fear. I don't know what I *don't* see—what I *don't* fear!"

Mrs. Grose tried to keep up with me. "You mean you're afraid of seeing her again?"

"Oh, no; that's nothing—now!" Then I explained. "It's of *not* seeing her."

But my companion only looked wan. "I don't understand you."

"Why, it's that the child may keep it up—and that the child assuredly *will*—without my knowing it."

At the image of this possibility Mrs. Grose for a moment collapsed, yet presently to pull herself together again, as if from the positive force of the sense of what, should we yield an inch, there would really be to give way to. "Dear, dear—we must keep our heads! And after all, if she doesn't mind it—!" She even tried a grim joke. "Perhaps she likes it!"

"Likes *such* things—a scrap of an infant!"

"Isn't it just a proof of her blessed innocence?" my friend bravely inquired.

She brought me, for the instant, almost round. "Oh, we must clutch at *that*—we must cling to it! If it isn't a proof of what you say, it's a proof of—God knows what! For the woman's a horror of horrors."

Mrs. Grose, at this, fixed her eyes a minute on the ground; then at last raising them, "Tell me how you know," she said.

"Then you admit it's what she was?" I cried.

"Tell me how you know," my friend simply repeated.

"Know! By seeing her! By the way she looked."

"At you, do you mean—so wickedly?"

"Dear me, no—I could have borne that. She gave me never a glance. She only fixed the child."

Mrs. Grose tried to see it. "Fixed her?"

"Ah, with such awful eyes!"

She stared at mine as if they might really have resembled them. "Do you mean of dislike?"

"God help us, no. Of something much worse."

"Worse than dislike?"—this left her indeed at a loss.

"With a determination—indescribable. With a kind of ry of intention."

I made her turn pale. "Intention?"

"To get hold of her." Mrs. Grose—her eyes just lingerg on mine—gave a shudder and walked to the window; d while she stood there looking out I completed my atement. "*That's* what Flora knows."

After a little she turned round. "The person was in ack, you say?"

"In mourning—rather poor, almost shabby. But—yes— ith extraordinary beauty." I now recognised to what I d at last, stroke by stroke, brought the victim of my conlence, for she quite visibly weighed this. "Oh, handsome very, very," I insisted; "wonderfully handsome. But inmous."

She slowly came back to me. "Miss Jessel—*was* inmous." She once more took my hand in both her own, lding it as tight as if to fortify me against the increase alarm I might draw from this disclosure. "They were th infamous," she finally said.

So, for a little, we faced it once more together; and I und absolutely a degree of help in seeing it now so raight. "I appreciate," I said, "the great decency of your t having hitherto spoken; but the time has certainly me to give me the whole thing." She appeared to assent this, but still only in silence; seeing which I went on: must have it now. Of what did she die? Come, there as something between them."

"There was everything."

"In spite of the difference—?"

"Oh, of their rank, their condition"—she brought it woelly out. "*She* was a lady."

I turned it over; I again saw. "Yes—she was a lady."

"And he so dreadfully below," said Mrs. Grose.

I felt that I doubtless needn't press too hard, in su
company, on the place of a servant in the scale; but the
was nothing to prevent an acceptance of my companio
own measure of my predecessor's abasement. There w
a way to deal with that, and I dealt; the more readily f
my full vision—on the evidence—of our employer's la
clever, good-looking "own" man; impudent, assure
spoiled, depraved. "The fellow was a hound."

Mrs. Grose considered as if it were perhaps a little
case for a sense of shades. "I've never seen one like hi
He did what he wished."

"With *her?*"

"With them all."

It was as if now in my friend's own eyes Miss Jessel h
again appeared. I seemed at any rate, for an instant,
see their evocation of her as distinctly as I had seen her
the pond; and I brought out with decision: "It must ha
been also what *she* wished!"

Mrs. Grose's face signified that it had been indeed, b
she said at the same time: "Poor woman—she paid for i

"Then you do know what she died of?" I asked.

"No—I know nothing. I wanted not to know; I was gl
enough I didn't; and I thanked heaven she was well o
of this!"

"Yet you had, then, your idea—"

"Of her real reason for leaving? Oh, yes—as to th
She couldn't have stayed. Fancy it here—for a governe
And afterwards I imagined—and I still imagine. And wh
I imagine is dreadful."

"Not so dreadful as what *I* do," I replied; on which
must have shown her—as I was indeed but too conscio
—a front of miserable defeat. It brought out again all h
compassion for me, and at the renewed touch of her kin
ness my power to resist broke down. I burst, as I had, t
other time, made her burst, into tears; she took me to h
motherly breast, and my lamentation overflowed. "I do

o it!" I sobbed in despair; "I don't save or shield them.
's far worse than I dreamed—they're lost!"

8

'HAT I HAD SAID TO MRS. GROSE was true enough: there
ere in the matter I had put before her depths and possi-
lities that I lacked resolution to sound; so that when we
et once more in the wonder of it we were of a common
ind about the duty of resistance to extravagant fancies.
'e were to keep our heads if we should keep nothing else
lifficult indeed as that might be in the face of what, in
ur prodigious experience, was least to be questioned. Late
at night, while the house slept, we had another talk in
y room, when she went all the way with me as to its
ing beyond doubt that I had seen exactly what I had
en. To hold her perfectly in the pinch of that, I found
ad only to ask her how, if I had "made it up," I came to
 able to give, of each of the persons appearing to me, a
cture disclosing, to the last detail, their special marks—
 portrait on the exhibition of which she had instantly
cognised and named them. She wished, of course,—small
ame to her!—to sink the whole subject; and I was quick
 assure her that my own interest in it had now violently
ken the form of a search for the way to escape from it. I
countered her on the ground of a probability that with
currence—for recurrence we took for granted—I should
t used to my danger, distinctly professing that my per-
nal exposure had suddenly become the least of my dis-
mforts. It was my new suspicion that was intolerable;
d yet even to this complication the later hours of the
y had brought a little ease.

On leaving her, after my first outbreak, I had of course
turned to my pupils, associating the right remedy for
y dismay with that sense of their charm which I had
ready found to be a thing I could positively cultivate

51

and which had never failed me yet. I had simply, in oth
words, plunged afresh into Flora's special society and the
become aware—it was almost a luxury!—that she cou
put her little conscious hand straight upon the spot th
ached. She had looked at me in sweet speculation and th
had accused me to my face of having "cried." I had su
posed I had brushed away the ugly signs: but I cou
literally—for the time, at all events—rejoice, under tl
fathomless charity, that they had not entirely disappeare
To gaze into the depths of blue of the child's eyes a
pronounce their loveliness a trick of premature cunni
was to be guilty of cynicism in preference to which
naturally preferred to abjure my judgment and, so f
as might be, my agitation. I couldn't abjure for mere
wanting to, but I could repeat to Mrs. Grose—as I d
there, over and over, in the small hours—that with the
voices in the air, their pressure on one's heart and the
fragrant faces against one's cheek, everything fell to t'
ground but their incapacity and their beauty. It was
pity that, somehow, to settle this once for all, I had equal
to re-enumerate the signs of subtlety that, in the aft
noon, by the lake, had made a miracle of my show of se
possession. It was a pity to be obliged to re-investigate t
certitude of the moment itself and repeat how it had cor
to me as a revelation that the inconceivable communion
then surprised was a matter, for either party, of habit.
was a pity that I should have had to quaver out again t
reasons for my not having, in my delusion, so much
questioned that the little girl saw our visitant even as
actually saw Mrs. Grose herself, and that she wanted,
just so much as she did thus see, to make me suppose sl
didn't, and at the same time, without showing anythir
arrive at a guess as to whether I myself did! It was a pi
that I needed once more to describe the portentous litt
activity by which she sought to divert my attention—t
perceptible increase of movement, the greater intensi
of play, the singing, the gabbling of nonsense, and t'
invitation to romp.

Yet if I had not indulged, to prove there was nothing in in this review, I should have missed the two or three m elements of comfort that still remained to me. I should ot for instance have been able to asseverate to my friend at I was certain—which was so much to the good—that at least had not betrayed myself. I should not have been ompted, by stress of need, by desperation of mind,—I arce know what to call it,—to invoke such further aid to telligence as might spring from pushing my colleague irly to the wall. She had told me, bit by bit, under essure, a great deal; but a small shifty spot on the wrong le of it all still sometimes brushed my brow like the ing of a bat; and I remember how on this occasion—for e sleeping house and the concentration alike of our nger and our watch seemed to help—I felt the impor- nce of giving the last jerk to the curtain. "I don't lieve anything so horrible," I recollect saying; "no, t us put it definitely, my dear, that I don't. But if I did, u know, there's a thing I should require now, just with- t sparing you the least bit more—oh, not a scrap, come! to get out of you. What was it you had in mind when, our distress, before Miles came back, over the letter om his school, you said, under my insistence, that you dn't pretend for him that he had not literally *ever* been ad'? He was *not* literally 'ever,' in these weeks that I yself have lived with him and so closely watched him; he s been an imperturbable little prodigy of delightful, veable goodness. Therefore you might perfectly have ade the claim for him if you had not, as it happened, en an exception to take. What was your exception, and what passage in your personal observation of him did u refer?"

It was a dreadfully austere inquiry, but levity was not ur note, and, at any rate, before the grey dawn admon- ned us to separate I had got my answer. What my friend d had in mind proved to be immensely to the purpose. was neither more nor less than the circumstance that for period of several months Quint and the boy had been

perpetually together. It was in fact the very appropria
truth that she had ventured to criticise the propriety,
hint at the incongruity, of so close an alliance, and ev
to go so far on the subject as a frank overture to M
Jessel. Miss Jessel had, with a most strange manner, n
quested her to mind her business, and the good wom
had, on this, directly approached little Miles. What s
had said to him, since I pressed, was that *she* liked to s
young gentlemen not forget their station.

I pressed again, of course, at this. "You reminded hi
that Quint was only a base menial?"

"As you might say! And it was his answer, for one thir
that was bad."

"And for another thing?" I waited. "He repeated yo
words to Quint?"

"No, not that. It's just what he *wouldn't!*" she cou
still impress upon me. "I was sure, at any rate," she adde
"that he didn't. But he denied certain occasions."

"What occasions?"

"When they had been about together quite as if Qui
were his tutor—and a very grand one—and Miss Jes
only for the little lady. When he had gone off with t
fellow, I mean, and spent hours with him."

"He then prevaricated about it—he said he hadn't?" H
assent was clear enough to cause me to add in a momer
"I see. He lied."

"Oh!" Mrs. Grose mumbled. This was a suggestion th
it didn't matter; which indeed she backed up by a furth
remark. "You see, after all, Miss Jessel didn't mind. S
didn't forbid him."

I considered. "Did he put that to you as a justificatior

At this she dropped again. "No, he never spoke of i

"Never mentioned her in connection with Quint?"

She saw, visibly flushing, where I was coming o
"Well, he didn't show anything. He denied," she repeate
"he denied."

Lord, how I pressed her now! "So that you could s
he knew what was between the two wretches?"

"I don't know—I don't know!" the poor woman groaned.

"You do know, you dear thing," I replied; "only you haven't my dreadful boldness of mind, and you keep back, out of timidity and modesty and delicacy, even the impression that, in the past, when you had, without my aid, to flounder about in silence, most of all made you miserable. But I shall get it out of you yet! There was something in the boy that suggested to you," I continued, "that he covered and concealed their relation."

"Oh, he couldn't prevent—"

"Your learning the truth? I dare say! But, heavens," I fell, with vehemence, a-thinking, "what it shows that they must, to that extent, have succeeded in making of him!"

"Ah nothing that's not nice *now!*" Mrs. Grose lugubriously pleaded.

"I don't wonder you looked queer," I persisted, "when I mentioned to you the letter from his school!"

"I doubt if I looked as queer as you!" she retorted with homely force. "And if he was so bad then as that comes to, how is he such an angel now?"

"Yes, indeed—and if he was a fiend at school! How, how, how? Well," I said in my torment, "you must put it to me again, but I shall not be able to tell you for some days. Only, put it to me again!" I cried in a way that made my friend stare. "There are directions in which I must not for the present let myself go." Meanwhile I returned to her first example—the one to which she had just previously referred—of the boy's happy capacity for an occasional slip. "If Quint—on your remonstrance at the time you speak of—was a base menial, one of the things Miles said to you, I find myself guessing, was that you were another." Again her admission was so adequate that I continued: "And you forgave him that?"

"Wouldn't *you?*"

"Oh, yes!" And we exchanged there, in the stillness, a sound of the oddest amusement. Then I went on: "At all events, while he was with the man—"

"Miss Flora was with the woman. It suited them all!"

It suited me too, I felt, only too well; by which I mean
that it suited exactly the particularly deadly view I was
in the very act of forbidding myself to entertain. But I
so far succeeded in checking the expression of this view
that I will throw, just here, no further light on it than
may be offered by the mention of my final observation to
Mrs. Grose. "His having lied and been impudent are, I
confess, less engaging specimens than I had hoped to
have from you of the outbreak in him of the little natural
man. Still," I mused, "they must do, for they make me
feel more than ever that I must watch."

It made me blush, the next minute, to see in my friend's
face how much more unreservedly she had forgiven him
than her anecdote struck me as presenting to my own
tenderness an occasion for doing. This came out when, at
the schoolroom door, she quitted me. "Surely you don't
accuse *him*—"

"Of carrying on an intercourse that he conceals from
me? Ah, remember that, until further evidence, I now
accuse nobody." Then, before shutting her out to go, by
another passage, to her own place, "I must just wait," I
wound up.

9

I WAITED AND WAITED, and the days, as they elapsed, took
something from my consternation. A very few of them, in
fact, passing, in constant sight of my pupils, without a
fresh incident, sufficed to give to grievous fancies and even
to odious memories a kind of brush of the sponge. I have
spoken of the surrender to their extraordinary childish
grace as a thing I could actively cultivate, and it may be
imagined if I neglected now to address myself to this
source for whatever it would yield. Stranger than I can
express, certainly, was the effort to struggle against my

ew lights; it would doubtless have been however, a
reater tension still had it not been so frequently success-
ul. I used to wonder how my little charges could help
uessing that I thought strange things about them; and the
rcumstance that these things only made them more in-
resting was not by itself a direct aid to keeping them
a the dark. I trembled lest they should see that they *were*
 immensely more interesting. Putting things at the worst,
t all events, as in meditation I so often did, any clouding
f their innocence could only be—blameless and fore-
oomed as they were—a reason the more for taking risks.
'here were moments when, by an irresistible impulse, I
und myself catching them up and pressing them to my
eart. As soon as I had done so I used to say to myself:
What will they think of that? Doesn't it betray too
uch?" It would have been easy to get into a sad, wild
ngle about how much I might betray; but the real ac-
unt, I feel, of the hours of peace that I could still enjoy
as that the immediate charm of my companions was a be-
uilement still effective even under the shadow of the
ossibility that it was studied. For if it occurred to me that
 might occasionally excite suspicion by the little out-
reaks of my sharper passion for them, so too I remember
ondering if I mightn't see a queerness in the traceable
ncrease of their own demonstrations.

They were at this period extravagantly and preternatur-
lly fond of me; which, after all, I could reflect, was no
ore than a graceful response in children perpetually
wed over and hugged. The homage of which they were
 lavish succeeded, in truth, for my nerves, quite as well
s if I never appeared to myself, as I may say, literally to
tch them at a purpose in it. They had never, I think,
anted to do so many things for their poor protectress; I
ean—though they got their lessons better and better,
hich was naturally what would please her most—in the
ay of diverting, entertaining, surprising her; reading
er passages, telling her stories, acting her charades, pounc-
g out at her, in disguises, as animals and historical char-

acters, and above all astonishing her by the "pieces" th
had secretly got by heart and could interminably recite.
should never get to the bottom—were I to let myself g
even now—of the prodigious private commentary, a
under still more private correction, with which, in the
days, I overscored their full hours. They had shown n
from the first a facility for everything, a general facul
which, taking a fresh start, achieved remarkable fligh
They got their little tasks as if they loved them, and i
dulged, from the mere exuberance of the gift, in the mo
unimposed little miracles of memory. They not on
popped out at me as tigers and as Romans, but as Shak
speareans, astronomers, and navigators. This was so si
gularly the case that it had presumably much to do wi
the fact as to which, at the present day, I am at a loss fe
a different explanation: I allude to my unnatural con
posure on the subject of another school for Miles. What
remember is that I was content not, for the time, to ope
the question, and that contentment must have sprur
from the sense of his perpetually striking show of cleve
ness. He was too clever for a bad governess, for a parson
daughter, to spoil; and the strangest if not the brighte
thread in the pensive embroidery I just spoke of was th
impression I might have got, if I had dared to work it ou
that he was under some influence operating in his sma
intellectual life as a tremendous incitement.

If it was easy to reflect, however, that such a boy cou
postpone school, it was at least as marked that for such
boy to have been "kicked out" by a school-master was
mystification without end. Let me add that in their cor
pany now—and I was careful almost never to be out of
—I could follow no scent very far. We lived in a cloud
music and love and success and private theatricals. Tl
musical sense in each of the children was of the quicke
but the elder in especial had a marvellous knack of catc
ing and repeating. The schoolroom piano broke into a
gruesome fancies; and when that failed there were confa
ulations in corners, with a sequel of one of them goir

out in the highest spirits in order to "come in" as something new. I had had brothers myself, and it was no revelation to me that little girls could be slavish idolaters of little boys. What surpassed everything was that there was a little boy in the world who could have for the inferior age, sex, and intelligence so fine a consideration. They were extraordinarily at one, and to say that they never either quarrelled or complained is to make the note of praise coarse for their quality of sweetness. Sometimes, indeed, when I dropped into coarseness, I perhaps came across traces of little understandings between them by which one of them should keep me occupied while the other slipped away. There is a *naïf* side, I suppose, in all diplomacy; but if my pupils practised upon me, it was surely with the minimum of grossness. It was all in the other quarter that, after a lull, the grossness broke out.

I find that I really hang back; but I must take my plunge. In going on with the record of what was hideous at Bly, I not only challenge the most liberal faith—for which I little care; but—and this is another matter—I renew what I myself suffered, I again push my way through it to the end. There came suddenly an hour after which, as I look back, the affair seems to me to have been all pure suffering; but I have at least reached the heart of it, and the straightest road out is doubtless to advance. One evening—with nothing to lead up or to prepare it—I felt the cold touch of the impression that had breathed on me the night of my arrival and which, much lighter then, as I have mentioned, I should probably have made little of in memory had my subsequent sojourn been less agitated. I had not gone to bed; I sat reading by a couple of candles. There was a roomful of old books at Bly—last-century fiction, some of it, which, to the extent of a distinctly deprecated renown, but never to so much as that of a stray specimen, had reached the sequestered home and appealed to the unavowed curiosity of my youth. I remember that the book I had in my hand was Fielding's *Amelia;* also that I was wholly awake. I recall further both a general conviction that it was horribly late and a particular objection to looking at my watch. I figure, finally, that the white curtain draping, in the fashion of those days, the head of Flora's little bed, shrouded, as I had assured myself long before, the perfection of childish rest. I recollect in short that, though I was deeply interested in my author, I found myself, at the turn of a page and with his spell all scattered, looking straight up from him and hard at the door of my room. There was a moment during which I listened, reminded of the faint sense I had had, the first night, of there being something undefineably astir in the house, and noted the soft breath of the open casement just move the half-drawn blind. Then, with all the marks of a deliberation that must have seemed magnificent had there been anyone to admire it, I laid down my book, rose to my feet, and, taking a candle, went straight out of the room and, from the passage, on which my light made little impression, noiselessly closed and locked the door.

I can say now neither what determined nor what guided me, but I went straight along the lobby, holding my candle high, till I came within sight of the tall window that presided over the great turn of the staircase. At this point I precipitately found myself aware of three things. They were practically simultaneous, yet they had flashes of succession. My candle, under a bold flourish, went out, and I perceived, by the uncovered window, that the yielding dusk of earliest morning rendered it unnecessary. Without it, the next instant, I saw that there was someone on the stair. I speak of sequences, but I required no lapse of seconds to stiffen myself for a third encounter with Quint. The apparition had reached the landing halfway up and was therefore on the spot nearest the window, where at sight of me, it stopped short and fixed me exactly as it had fixed me from the tower and from the garden. He knew me as well as I knew him; and so, in the cold, faint twilight, with a glimmer in the high glass and another on the polish of the oak stair below, we faced each other in our common intensely. He was absolutely, on this occasion, a living, detestable, dangerous presence. But that was not the wonder of wonders; I reserve this distinction for quite another circumstance: the circumstance that dread had unmistakably quitted me and that there was nothing in me there that didn't meet and measure him.

I had plenty of anguish after that extraordinary moment, but I had, thank God, no terror. And he knew I had not—I found myself at the end of an instant magnificently aware of this. I felt, in a fierce rigour of confidence, that if I stood my ground a minute I should cease —for the time, at least—to have him to reckon with; and during the minute, accordingly, the thing was as human and hideous as a real interview: hideous just because it *was* human, as human as to have met alone, in the small hours, in a sleeping house, some enemy, some adventurer, some criminal. It was the dead silence of our long gaze at such close quarters that gave the whole horror, huge as it was, its only note of the unnatural. If I had met a murderer in such a place and at such an hour, we still at least would have spoken. Something would have passed, in life, between us; if nothing had passed one of us would have moved. The moment was so prolonged that it would have taken but little more to make me doubt if even I were in life. I can't express what followed it save by saying that the silence itself—which was indeed in a manner an attestation of my strength—became the element into which I saw the figure disappear; in which I definitely saw it turn as I might have seen the low wretch to which it had once belonged turn on receipt of an order, and pass, with my eyes on the villainous back that no hunch could have more disfigured, straight down the staircase and into the darkness in which the next bend was lost.

10

I REMAINED AWHILE at the top of the stair, but with the effect presently of understanding that when my visitor had gone, he had gone: then I returned to my room. The foremost thing I saw there by the light of the candle I had left burning was that Flora's little bed was empty; and on this I caught my breath with all the terror that, five minutes before, I had been able to resist. I dashed at the place in which I had left her lying and over which (for the small silk counterpane and the sheets were disarranged) the white curtains had been deceivingly pulled forward; then my step, to my unutterable relief, produced an answering sound: I perceived an agitation of the window-blind, and the child, ducking down, emerged rosily from the other side of it. She stood there in so much of her candour and so little of her nightgown, with her pink bare feet and the golden glow of her curls. She looked intensely grave, and I had never had such a sense of losing an advantage acquired (the thrill of which had just been so prodigious) as on my consciousness that she addressed me with a reproach. "You naughty: where *have* you been?" —instead of challenging her own irregularity I found myself arraigned and explaining. She herself explained, for that matter, with the loveliest, eagerest simplicity. She had known suddenly, as she lay there, that I was out of the room, and had jumped up to see what had become of me. I had dropped, with the joy of her reappearance, back into my chair—feeling then, and then only, a little faint; and she had pattered straight over to me, thrown herself upon my knee, given herself to be held with the flame of the candle full in the wonderful little face that was still flushed with sleep. I remember closing my eyes an instant, yielding, consciously, as before the excess of something beautiful that shone out of the blue of her own.

"You were looking for me out of the window?" I said. "You thought I might be walking in the grounds?"

"Well, you know, I thought someone was"—she never blanched as she smiled out that at me.

Oh, how I looked at her now! "And did you see anyone?"

"Ah, *no!*" she returned, almost with the full privilege of childish inconsequence, resentfully, though with a long sweetness in her little drawl of the negative.

At that moment, in the state of my nerves, I absolutely believed she lied; and if I once more closed my eyes it was before the dazzle of the three or four possible ways in which I might take this up. One of these, for a moment, tempted me with such singular intensity that, to withstand it, I must have gripped my little girl with a spasm that, wonderfully, she submitted to without a cry or a sign of fright. Why not break out at her on the spot and have it all over?—give it to her straight in her lovely little lighted face? "You see, you see, you *know* that you do and that you already quite suspect I believe it; therefore why not frankly confess it to me, so that we may at least live with it together and learn perhaps, in the strangeness of our fate, where we are and what it means?" This solicitation dropped, alas, as it came: if I could immediately have succumbed to it I might have spared myself—well you'll see what. Instead of succumbing I sprang again to my feet, looked at her bed, and took a helpless middle way. "Why did you pull the curtain over the place to make me think you were still there?"

Flora luminously considered; after which, with her little divine smile: "Because I don't like to frighten you!"

"But if I had, by your idea, gone out—?"

She absolutely declined to be puzzled; she turned her eyes to the flame of the candle as if the question were as irrelevant, or at any rate as impersonal, as Mrs. Marcet or nine-times-nine. "Oh, but you know," she quite adequately answered, "that you might come back, you dear, and that you *have!*" And after a little, when she had got into bed, I had, for a long time, by almost sitting on her to hold her hand, to prove that I recognised the pertinence of my return.

You may imagine the general complexion, from that moment, of my nights. I repeatedly sat up till I didn't know when; I selected moments when my room-mate unmistakeably slept, and, stealing out, took noiseless turns in the passage and even pushed as far as to where I had last met Quint. But I never met him there again; and I may as well say at once that I on no other occasion saw him in the house. I just missed, on the staircase, on the other hand, a different adventure. Looking down it from the top I once recognised the presence of a woman seated on one of the lower steps with her back presented to me, her body half bowed and her head, in an attitude of woe, in her hands. I had been there but an instant, however, when she vanished without looking round at me. I knew, none the less, exactly what dreadful face she had to show; and I wondered whether, if instead of being above I had been below, I should have had, for going up, the same nerve I had lately shown Quint. Well, there continued to be plenty of chance for nerve. On the eleventh night after my last encounter with that gentleman—they were all numbered now—I had an alarm that perilously skirted it and that indeed, from the particular quality of its unexpectedness, proved quite my sharpest shock. It was precisely the first night during this series that, weary with watching, I had felt that I might again without laxity lay myself down at my old hour. I slept immediately and, as I afterwards knew, till about one o'clock; but when I woke it was to sit straight up, as completely roused as if a hand had shook me. I had left a light burning, but it was now out, and I felt an instant certainty that Flora had extinguished it. This brought me to my feet and straight, in the darkness, to her bed, which I found she had left. A glance at the window enlightened me further, and the striking of a match completed the picture.

The child had again got up—this time blowing out the

taper, and had again, for some purpose of observation or response, squeezed in behind the blind and was peering out into the night. That she now saw—as she had not, I had satisfied myself, the previous time—was proved to me by the fact that she was disturbed neither by my re-illumination nor by the haste I made to get into slippers and into a wrap. Hidden, protected, absorbed, she evidently rested on the sill—the casement opened forward—and gave herself up. There was a great still moon to help her, and this fact had counted in my quick decision. She was face to face with the apparition we had met at the lake, and could now communicate with it as she had not then been able to do. What I, on my side, had to care for was, without disturbing her, to reach, from the corridor, some other window in the same quarter. I got to the door without her hearing me; I got out of it, closed it and listened, from the other side, for some sound from her. While I stood in the passage I had my eyes on her brother's door, which was but ten steps off and which, indescribably, produced in me a renewal of the strange impulse that I lately spoke of as my temptation. What if I should go straight in and march to *his* window?—what if, by risking to his boyish bewilderment a revelation of my motive, I should throw across the rest of the mystery the long halter of my boldness?

This thought held me sufficiently to make me cross to his threshold and pause again. I preternaturally listened; I figured to myself what might portentously be; I wondered if his bed were also empty and he too were secretly at watch. It was a deep, soundless minute, at the end of which my impulse failed. He was quiet; he might be innocent; the risk was hideous; I turned away. There was a figure in the grounds—a figure prowling for a sight, the visitor with whom Flora was engaged; but it was not the visitor most concerned with my boy. I hesitated afresh, but on other grounds and only a few seconds; then I had made my choice. There were empty rooms at Bly, and it was only a question of choosing the right one. The right one suddenly presented itself to me as the lower one—though high above the gardens—in the solid corner of the house that I have spoken of as the old tower. This was a large, square chamber, arranged with some state as a bed-room, the extravagant size of which made it so inconvenient that it had not for years, though kept by Mrs. Grose in exemplary order, been occupied. I had often admired it and I knew my way about in it; I had only after just faltering at the first chill gloom of its disuse, to pass across it and unbolt as quietly as I could one of the shutters. Achieving this transit, I uncovered the glass without a sound and, applying my face to the pane, was able, the darkness without being much less than within, to see that I commanded the right direction. Then I saw something more. The moon made the night extraordinarily penetrable and showed me on the lawn a person, diminished by distance, who stood there motionless and as if fascinated, looking up to where I had appeared—looking, that is, not so much straight at me as at something that was apparently above me. There was clearly another person above me—there was a person on the tower; but the presence on the lawn was not in the least what I had conceived and had confidently hurried to meet. The presence on the lawn—I felt sick as I made it out—was poor little Miles himself.

11

IT WAS NOT TILL LATE NEXT DAY that I spoke to Mrs. Grose; the rigour with which I kept my pupils in sight making it often difficult to meet her privately, and the more as we each felt the importance of not provoking—on the part of the servants quite as much as on that of the children—any suspicion of a secret flurry or of a discussion of mysteries. I drew a great security in this particular from her mere smooth aspect. There was nothing in her fresh face

pass on to others my horrible confidences. She believed
e, I was sure, absolutely: if she hadn't I don't know
hat would have become of me, for I couldn't have borne
e business alone. But she was a magnificent monument
the blessing of a want of imagination, and if she could
e in our little charges nothing but their beauty and
niability, their happiness and cleverness, she had no
rect communication with the sources of my trouble. If
ey had been at all visibly blighted or battered, she
ould doubtless have grown, on tracing it back, haggard
ough to match them; as matters stood, however, I could
el her, when she surveyed them, with her large white
ms folded and the habit of serenity in all her look,
ank the Lord's mercy that if they were ruined the pieces
ould still serve. Flights of fancy gave place, in her mind,
a steady fireside glow, and I had already begun to
rceive how, with the development of the conviction that
as time went on without a public accident—our young
ings could, after all, look out for themselves, she ad-
essed her greatest solicitude to the sad case presented
their instructress. That, for myself, was a sound simpli-
ation: I could engage that, to the world, my face should
ll no tales, but it would have been, in the conditions, an
mense added strain to find myself anxious about hers.
At the hour I now speak of she had joined me, under
essure, on the terrace, where, with the lapse of the
ason, the afternoon sun was now agreeable; and we sat
ere together while, before us, at a distance, but within
ll if we wished, the children strolled to and fro in one
their most manageable moods. They moved slowly, in
ison, below us, over the lawn, the boy, as they went,
ading aloud from a storybook and passing his arm
und his sister to keep her quite in touch. Mrs. Grose
tched them with positive placidity; then I caught the
ppressed intellectual creak with which she conscien-
ously turned to take from me a view of the back of the
pestry. I had made her a receptacle of lurid things, but
ere was an odd recognition of my superiority—my ac-

complishments and my function—in her patience und
my pain. She offered her mind to my disclosures as, had
wished to mix a witch's broth and proposed it with ;
surance, she would have held out a large clean saucepa
This had become thoroughly her attitude by the tir
that, in my recital of the events of the night, I reached tl
point of what Miles had said to me when, after seeir
him, at such a monstrous hour, almost on the very sp
where he happened now to be, I had gone down to bri
him in; choosing then, at the window, with a concentrat
need of not alarming the house, rather that method tha
a signal more resonant. I had left her meanwhile in litt
doubt of my small hope of representing with success ev
to her actual sympathy my sense of the real splendour
the little inspiration with which, after I had got him in
the house, the boy met my final articulate challenge. ,
soon as I appeared in the moonlight on the terrace, l
had come to me as straight as possible; on which I h;
taken his hand without a word and led him, through tl
dark spaces, up the staircase where Quint had so hungri
hovered for him, along the lobby where I had listen
and trembled, and so to his forsaken room.

Not a sound, on the way, had passed between us, ar
I had wondered—oh, *how* I had wondered!—if he we
groping about in his little mind for something plausil
and not too grotesque. It would tax his invention, c
tainly, and I felt, this time, over his real embarrassment
curious thrill of triumph. It was a sharp trap for t
inscrutable! He couldn't play any longer at innocence;
how the deuce would he get out of it? There beat in r
indeed, with the passionate throb of this question, ;
equal dumb appeal as to how the deuce *I* should. I w
confronted at last, as never yet, with all the risk attach
even now to sounding my own hurried note. I rememb
in fact that as we pushed into his little chamber, whe
the bed had not been slept in at all and the window, u
covered to the moonlight, made the place so clear th
there was no need of striking a match—I remember h

suddenly dropped, sank upon the edge of the bed from the force of the idea that he must know how he really, as they say, "had" me. He could do what he liked, with all his cleverness to help him, so long as I should continue to defer to the old tradition of the criminality of those caretakers of the young who minister to superstitions and fears. He "had" me indeed, and in a cleft stick; for who would ever absolve me, who would consent that I should go unhung, if, by the faintest tremor of an overture, I were the first to introduce into our perfect intercourse an element so dire? No, no: it was useless to attempt to convey to Mrs. Grose, just as it is scarcely less so to attempt to suggest here, how, in our short, stiff brush in the dark, he fairly shook me with admiration. I was of course thoroughly kind and merciful; never, never yet had I placed on his little shoulders hands of such tenderness as those with which, while I rested against the bed, I held him there well under fire. I had no alternative but, in form at least, to put it to him.

"You must tell me now—and all the truth. What did you go out for? What were you doing there?"

I can still see his wonderful smile, the whites of his beautiful eyes, and the uncovering of his little teeth shine to me in the dusk. "If I tell you why, will you understand?" My heart, at this, leaped into my mouth. *Would* he tell me why? I found no sound on my lips to press it, and I was aware of replying only with a vague, repeated, grimacing nod. He was gentleness itself, and while I wagged my head at him he stood there more than ever a little fairy prince. It was his brightness indeed that gave me a respite. Would it be so great if he were really going to tell me? "Well," he said at last, "just exactly in order that you should do this."

"Do what?"

"Think me—for a change—*bad!*" I shall never forget the sweetness and gaiety with which he brought out the word, nor how, on top of it, he bent forward and kissed me. It was practically the end of everything. I met his kiss

69

and I had to make, while I folded him for a minute in m
arms, the most stupendous effort not to cry. He had give
exactly the account of himself that permitted least of m
going behind it, and it was only with the effect of cor
firming my acceptance of it that, as I presently glance
about the room, I could say—

"Then you didn't undress at all?"

He fairly glittered in the gloom. "Not at all. I sat up an
read."

"And when did you go down?"

"At midnight. When I'm bad I *am* bad!"

"I see, I see—it's charming. But how could you be sur
I would know it?"

"Oh, I arranged that with Flora." His answers ran
out with a readiness! "She was to get up and look out."

"Which is what she did do." It was I who fell into th
trap!

"So she disturbed you, and, to see what she was lookin
at, you also looked—you saw."

"While you," I concurred, "caught your death in th
night air!"

He literally bloomed so from this exploit that he coul
afford radiantly to assent. "How otherwise should I hav
been bad enough?" he asked. Then, after another em
brace, the incident and our interview closed on my reco
nition of all the reserves of goodness that, for his joke, h
had been able to draw upon.

12

THE PARTICULAR IMPRESSION I had received proved in th
morning light, I repeat, not quite successfully presentab
to Mrs. Grose, though I reinforced it with the mention
still another remark that he had made before we sep
rated. "It all lies in half-a-dozen words," I said to he
"words that really settle the matter. 'Think, you kno

hat I *might* do!' He threw that off to show me how good
e is. He knows down to the ground what he 'might' do.
'hat's what he gave them a taste of at school."

"Lord, you do change!" cried my friend.

"I don't change—I simply make it out. The four, de-
end upon it, perpetually meet. If on either of these
st nights you had been with either child, you would
early have understood. The more I've watched and
aited the more I've felt that if there were nothing
se to make it sure it would be made so by the systematic
lence of each. *Never,* by a slip of the tongue, have they
much as alluded to either of their old friends, any more
an Miles has alluded to his expulsion. Oh yes, we may
t here and look at them, and they may show off to us there
their fill; but even while they pretend to be lost in their
iry-tale they're steeped in their vision of the dead re-
ored. He's not reading to her," I declared; "they're talk-
g of *them*—they're talking horrors! I go on, I know, as if
were crazy; and it's a wonder I'm not. What I've seen
ould have made *you* so; but it has only made me more
cid, made me get hold of still other things."

My lucidity must have seemed awful, but the charm-
g creatures who were victims of it, passing and repass-
g in their interlocked sweetness, gave my colleague
mething to hold on by; and I felt how tight she held as,
ithout stirring in the breath of my passion, she covered
em still with her eyes. "Of what other things have you
t hold?"

"Why, of the very things that have delighted, fasci-
ated, and yet, at bottom, as I now so strangely see, mysti-
d and troubled me. Their more than earthly beauty,
eir absolutely unnatural goodness. It's a game," I went
; "it's a policy and a fraud!"

"On the part of little darlings—?"

"As yet mere lovely babies? Yes, mad as that seems!"
he very act of bringing it out really helped me to trace
—follow it all up and piece it all together. "They haven't
en good—they've only been absent. It has been easy to

71

live with them, because they're simply leading a life
their own. They're not mine—they're not ours. They
his and they're hers!"

"Quint's and that woman's?"

"Quint's and that woman's. They want to get to then

Oh, how, at this, poor Mrs. Grose appeared to stu
them! "But for what?"

"For the love of all the evil that, in those dreadful da
the pair put into them. And to ply them with that e
still, to keep up the work of demons, is what brings t
others back."

"Laws!" said my friend under her breath. The exc
mation was homely, but it revealed a real acceptance
my further proof of what, in the bad time—for there h
been a worse even than this!—must have occurred. The
could have been no such justification for me as the pl
assent of her experience to whatever depth of deprav
I found credible in our brace of scoundrels. It was in
vious submission of memory that she brought out afte
moment: "They *were* rascals! But what can they now d
she pursued.

"Do?" I echoed so loud that Miles and Flora, as th
passed at their distance, paused an instant in their w
and looked at us. "Don't they do enough?" I demanded
a lower tone, while the children, having smiled and nod
and kissed hands to us, resumed their exhibition. We w
held by it a minute; then I answered: "They can dest
them!" At this my companion did turn, but the inqu
she launched was a silent one, the effect of which was
make me more explicit. "They don't know, as yet, qu
how—but they're trying hard. They're seen only acr
as it were, and beyond—in strange places and on h
places, the top of towers, the roof of houses, the outs
of windows, the further edge of pools; but there's a d
design, on either side, to shorten the distance and ov
come the obstacle; and the success of the tempters is o
a question of time. They've only to keep to their s
gestions of danger."

"For the children to come?"

"And perish in the attempt!" Mrs. Grose slowly got up, and I scrupulously added: "Unless, of course, we can prevent!"

Standing there before me while I kept my seat, she visibly turned things over. "Their uncle must do the preventing. He must take them away."

"And who's to make him?"

She had been scanning the distance, but she now dropped on me a foolish face. "You, Miss."

"By writing to him that his house is poisoned and his little nephew and niece mad?"

"But if they *are*, Miss?"

"And if I am myself, you mean? That's charming news to be sent him by a governess whose prime undertaking was to give him no worry."

Mrs. Grose considered, following the children again. "Yes, he do hate worry. That was the great reason—"

"Why those fiends took him in so long? No doubt, though his indifference must have been awful. As I'm not a fiend, at any rate, I shouldn't take him in."

My companion, after an instant and for all answer, sat down again and grasped my arm. "Make him at any rate come to you."

I stared. "To *me?*" I had a sudden fear of what she might do. " 'Him'?"

"He ought to *be* here—he ought to help."

I quickly rose, and I think I must have shown her a queerer face than ever yet. "You see me asking him for a visit?" No, with her eyes on my face she evidently couldn't. Instead of it even—as a woman reads another—she could see what I myself saw: his derision, his amusement, his contempt for the break-down of my resignation at being left alone and for the fine machinery I had set in motion to attract his attention to my slighted charms. She didn't know—no one knew—how proud I had been to serve him and to stick to our terms; yet she none the less took the measure, I think, of the warning I now gave her. "If you

should so lose your head as to appeal to him for me—"
She was really frightened. "Yes, Miss?"
"I would leave, on the spot, both him and you."

IT WAS ALL VERY WELL to join them, but speaking to them
proved quite as much as ever an effort beyond my strength
—offered, in close quarters, difficulties as insurmountable
as before. This situation continued a month, and with
new aggravations and particular notes, the note above all,
sharper and sharper, of the small ironic consciousness on
the part of my pupils. It was not, I am as sure today as I
was sure then, my mere infernal imagination: it was absolutely traceable that they were aware of my predicament
and that this strange relation made, in a manner, for a
long time, the air in which we moved. I don't mean that
they had their tongues in their cheeks or did anything vulgar, for that was not one of their dangers: I do mean, on
the other hand, that the element of the unnamed and
untouched became, between us, greater than any other
and that so much avoidance could not have been so successfully effected without a great deal of tacit arrangement.
It was as if, at moments, we were perpetually coming into
sight of subjects before which we must stop short, turning
suddenly out of alleys that we perceived to be blind, closing
with a little bang that made us look at each other—for
like all bangs, it was something louder than we had intended—the doors we had indiscreetly opened. All roads
lead to Rome, and there were times when it might have
struck us that almost every branch of study or subject of
conversation skirted forbidden ground. Forbidden ground
was the question of the return of the dead in general and
of whatever, in especial, might survive, in memory, of the
friends little children had lost. There were days when I
could have sworn that one of them had, with a small

invisible nudge, said to the other: "She thinks she'll do it this time—but she *won't!*" To "do it" would have been to indulge for instance—and for once in a way—in some direct reference to the lady who had prepared them for my discipline. They had a delightful endless appetite for passages in my own history, to which I had again and again treated them; they were in possession of everything that had ever happened to me, had had, with every circumstance, the story of my smallest adventures and of those of my brothers and sisters and of the cat and the dog at home, as well as many particulars of the eccentric nature of my father, of the furniture and arrangement of our house, and of the conversation of the old women of our village. There were things enough, taking one with another, to chatter about, if one went very fast and knew by instinct when to go round. They pulled with an art of their own the strings of my invention and my memory; and nothing else perhaps, when I thought of such occasions afterwards, gave me so the suspicion of being watched from under cover. It was in any case over *my* life, *my* past, and *my* friends alone that we could take anything like our ease— a state of affairs that led them sometimes without the least pertinence to break out into sociable reminders. I was invited—with no visible connection—to repeat afresh Goody Gosling's celebrated *mot* or to confirm the details already supplied as to the cleverness of the vicarage pony.

It was partly at such junctures as these and partly at quite different ones that, with the turn my matters had now taken, my predicament, as I have called it, grew most sensible. The fact that the days passed for me without another encounter ought, it would have appeared, to have done something toward soothing my nerves. Since the light brush, that second night on the upper landing, of the presence of a woman at the foot of the stair, I had seen nothing, whether in or out of the house, that one had better not have seen. There was many a corner round which I expected to come upon Quint, and many a situation that, in a merely sinister way, would have favoured

the appearance of Miss Jessel. The summer had turned
the summer had gone; the autumn had dropped upon Bl
and had blown out half our lights. The place, with it
grey sky and withered garlands, its bared spaces an
scattered dead leaves, was like a theatre after the per
formance—all strewn with crumpled playbills. There wer
exactly states of the air, conditions of sound and of stil
ness, unspeakable impressions of the *kind* of ministerin
moment, that brought back to me, long enough to catc
it, the feeling of the medium in which, that June evenin
out-of-doors, I had had my first sight of Quint, and i
which, too, at those other instants, I had, after seeing hir
through the window, looked for him in vain in the circl
of shrubbery. I recognised the signs, the portents—I recog
nised the moment, the spot. But they remained unaccom
panied and empty, and I continued unmolested; if unmo
lested one could call a young woman whose sensibilit
had, in the most extraordinary fashion, not declined bu
deepened. I had said in my talk with Mrs. Grose on tha
horrid scene of Flora's by the lake—and had perplexe
her by so saying—that it would from that moment distre
me much more to lose my power than to keep it. I had the
expressed what was vividly in my mind: the truth tha
whether the children really saw or not—since, that is,
was not yet definitely proved—I greatly preferred, as
safeguard, the fulness of my own exposure. I was read
to know the very worst that was to be known. What I ha
then had an ugly glimpse of was that my eyes might b
sealed just while theirs were most opened. Well, my ey
were sealed, it appeared, at present—a consummation fo
which it seemed blasphemous not to thank God. Ther
was, alas, a difficulty about that: I would have thanke
him with all my soul had I not had in a proportiona
measure this conviction of the secret of my pupils.

How can I retrace today the strange steps of my obse
sion? There were times of our being together when
would have been ready to swear that, literally, in m
presence, but with my direct sense of it closed, they ha

visitors who were known and were welcome. Then it was that, had I not been deterred by the very chance that such an injury might prove greater than the injury to be averted, my exultation would have broken out. "They're here, they're here, you little wretches," I would have cried, "and you can't deny it now!" The little wretches denied it with all the added volume of their sociability and their tenderness, in just the crystal depths of which—like the flash of a fish in a stream—the mockery of their advantage peeped up. The shock, in truth, had sunk into me still deeper than I knew on the night when, looking out to see either Quint or Miss Jessel under the stars, I had beheld the boy over whose rest I watched and who had immediately brought in with him—had straightway, there, turned it on me—the lovely upward look with which from the battlements above me, the hideous apparition of Quint had played. If it was a question of a scare, my discovery on this occasion had scared me more than any other, and it was in the condition of nerves produced by it that I made my actual inductions. They harassed me so that sometimes, at odd moments, I shut myself up audibly to rehearse—it was at once a fantastic relief and a renewed despair—the manner in which I might come to the point. I approached it from one side and the other while, in my room, I flung myself about, but I always broke down in the monstrous utterance of names. As they died away on my lips, I said to myself that I should indeed help them to represent something infamous if, by pronouncing them, I should violate as rare a little case of instinctive delicacy as any schoolroom, probably, had ever known. When I said to myself: "*They* have the manners to be silent, and you, trusted as you are, the baseness to speak!" I felt myself crimson and I covered my face with my hands. After these secret scenes I chattered more than ever, going on volubly enough 'til one of our prodigious, palpable hushes occurred—I can call them nothing else —the strange, dizzy lift or swim (I try for terms!) into a stillness, a pause of all life, that had nothing to do with the more or less noise that at the moment we might be engaged in making and that I could hear through any deepened exhilaration or quickened recitation or louder strum of the piano. Then it was that the others, the outsiders, were there. Though they were not angels, they "passed," as the French say, causing me, while they stayed, to tremble with the fear of their addressing to their younger victims some yet more infernal message or more vivid image than they had thought good enough for myself.

What it was most impossible to get rid of was the cruel idea that, whatever I had seen, Miles and Flora saw *more* —things terrible and unguessable and that sprang from dreadful passages of intercourse in the past. Such things naturally left on the surface, for the time, a chill which we vociferously denied that we felt; and we had, all three, with repetition, got into such splendid training that we went, each time, almost automatically, to mark the close of the incident, through the very same movements. It was striking of the children, at all events, to kiss me inveterately with a kind of wild irrelevance and never to fail— one or the other—of the precious question that had helped us through many a peril. "When do you think he *will* come? Don't you think we *ought* to write?"—there was nothing like that inquiry, we found by experience, for carrying off an awkwardness. "He" of course was their uncle in Harley Street; and we lived in much profusion of theory that he might at any moment arrive to mingle in our circle. It was impossible to have given less encouragement than he had done to such a doctrine, but if we had not had the doctrine to fall back upon we should have deprived each other of some of our finest exhibitions. He never wrote to them—that may have been selfish, but it was a part of the flattery of his trust of me; for the way in which a man pays his highest tribute to a woman is apt to be but by the more festal celebration of one of the sacred laws of his comfort; and I held that I carried out the spirit of the pledge given not to appeal to him when

let my charges understand that their own letters were but
charming literary exercises. They were too beautiful to be
posted; I kept them myself; I have them all to this hour.
This was a rule indeed which only added to the satiric
effect of my being plied with the supposition that he might
at any moment be among us. It was exactly as if my
charges knew how almost more awkward than anything
else that might be for me. There appears to me, moreover,
as I look back, no note in all this more extraordinary than
the mere fact that, in spite of my tension and of their
triumph, I never lost patience with them. Adorable they
must in truth have been, I now reflect, that I didn't in
these days hate them! Would exasperation, however, if
relief had longer been postponed, finally have betrayed
me? It little matters, for relief arrived. I call it relief,
though it was only the relief that a snap brings to a strain
or the burst of a thunderstorm to a day of suffocation. It
was at least change, and it came with a rush.

14

WALKING TO CHURCH a certain Sunday morning, I had
little Miles at my side and his sister, in advance of us and
with Mrs. Grose's, well in sight. It was a crisp, clear day, the
first of its order for some time; the night had brought a
touch of frost, and the autumn air, bright and sharp, made
the church-bells almost gay. It was an odd accident of
thought that I should have happened at such a moment
to be particularly and very gratefully struck with the
obedience of my little charges. Why did they never re-
sent my inexorable, my perpetual society? Something or
other had brought nearer home to me that I had all but
pinned the boy to my shawl and that, in the way our
companions were marshalled before me, I might have appeared to provide against some danger of rebellion. I was
like a gaoler with an eye to possible surprises and escapes.

But all this belonged—I mean their magnificent little su
render—just to the special array of the facts that were mo
abysmal. Turned out for Sunday by his uncle's tailor, wl
had had a free hand and a notion of pretty waistcoa
and of his grand little air, Miles's whole title to indepe
dence, the rights of his sex and situation, were so stampe
upon him that if he had suddenly struck for freedom
should have had nothing to say. I was by the strange
of chances wondering how I should meet him when tl
revolution unmistakeably occurred. I call it a revolutic
because I now see how, with the word he spoke, the cu
tain rose on the last act of my dreadful drama and tl
catastrophe was precipitated. "Look here, my dear, yc
know," he charmingly said, "when in the world, pleas
am I going back to school?"

Transcribed here the speech sounds harmless enoug
particularly as uttered in the sweet, high, casual pipe wi
which, at all interlocutors, but above all at his eternal go
erness, he threw off intonations as if he were tossing rose
There was something in them that always made or
"catch," and I caught, at any rate, now so effectually th
I stopped as short as if one of the trees of the park ha
fallen across the road. There was something new, on th
spot, between us, and he was perfectly aware that I reco
nized it, though, to enable me to do so, he had no nee
to look a whit less candid and charming than usual.
could feel in him how he already, from my at first findir
nothing to reply, perceived the advantage he had gaine
I was so slow to find anything that he had plenty of tim
after a minute, to continue with his suggestive but inco
clusive smile: "You know, my dear, that for a fellow to l
with a lady *always*—!" His "my dear" was constantly c
his lips for me, and nothing could have expressed mo
the exact shade of the sentiment with which I desired
inspire my pupils than its fond familiarity. It was so r
spectfully easy.

But, oh, how I felt that at present I must pick my ov
phrases! I remember that, to gain time, I tried to laug

nd I seemed to see in the beautiful face with which he
watched me how ugly and queer I looked. "And always
with the same lady?" I returned.

He neither blenched nor winked. The whole thing was
virtually out between us. "Ah, of course, she's a jolly,
perfect lady; but, after all, I'm a fellow, don't you see?
hat's—well, getting on."

I lingered there with him an instant ever so kindly.
Yes, you're getting on." Oh, but I felt helpless!

I have kept to this day the heartbreaking little idea of
ow he seemed to know that and to play with it. "And
ou can't say I've not been awfully good, can you?"

I laid my hand on his shoulder, for, though I felt how
nuch better it would have been to walk on, I was not yet
quite able. "No, I can't say that, Miles."

"Except just that one night, you know—!"

"That one night?" I couldn't look as straight as he.

"Why, when I went down—went out of the house."

"Oh, yes. But I forget what you did it for."

"You forget?"—he spoke with the sweet extravagance
f childish reproach. "Why, it was to show you I could!"

"Oh, yes, you could."

"And I can again."

I felt that I might, perhaps, after all succeed in keeping
y wits about me. "Certainly. But you won't."

"No, not *that* again. It was nothing."

"It was nothing," I said. "But we must go on."

He resumed our walk with me, passing his hand into my
rm. "Then when *am* I going back?"

I wore, in turning it over, my most responsible air.
Were you very happy at school?"

He just considered. "Oh, I'm happy enough anywhere!"

"Well, then," I quavered, "if you're just as happy
ere—!"

"Ah, but that isn't everything! Of course *you* know a
ot—"

"But you hint that you know almost as much?" I risked
s he paused.

"Not half I want to!" Miles honestly professed. "Bu it isn't so much that."

"What is it, then?"

"Well—I want to see more life."

"I see; I see." We had arrived within sight of the churcl and of various persons, including several of the house hold of Bly, on their way to it and clustered about th door to see us go in. I quickened our step; I wanted t get there before the question between us opened up mucl further; I reflected hungrily that, for more than an hou he would have to be silent; and I thought with envy of th comparative dusk of the pew and of the almost spiritua help of the hassock on which I might bend my knees. seemed literally to be running a race with some confusio to which he was about to reduce me, but I felt that he ha got in first when, before we had even entered the churcl yard, he threw out—

"I want my own sort!"

It literally made me bound forward. "There are no many of your own sort, Miles!" I laughed. "Unless pe haps dear little Flora!"

"You really compare me to a baby girl?"

This found me singularly weak. "Don't you, then, *lov* our sweet Flora?"

"If I didn't—and you too; if I didn't—!" he repeate as if retreating for a jump, yet leaving his thought so ur finished that, after we had come into the gate, anothe stop, which he imposed on me by the pressure of his arn had become inevitable. Mrs. Grose and Flora had passe into the church, the other worshippers had followed, an we were, for the minute, alone among the old, thic graves. We had paused, on the path from the gate, by low, oblong, table-like tomb.

"Yes. If you didn't—?"

He looked, while I waited, about at the graves. "Wel you know what!" But he didn't move, and he present produced something that made me drop straight dow on the stone slab, as if suddenly to rest. "Does my uncl nk what *you* think?"

markedly rested. "How do you know what I think?"

"Ah, well, of course I don't; for it strikes me you never
me. But I mean does *he* know?"

"Know what, Miles?"

"Why, the way I'm going on."

perceived quickly enough that I could make, to this
uiry, no answer that would not involve something of a
rifice of my employer. Yet it appeared to me that we
re all, at Bly, sufficiently sacrificed to make that venial.
don't think your uncle much cares."

Miles, on this, stood looking at me. "Then don't you
nk he can be made to?"

"In what way?"

"Why, by his coming down."

"But who'll get him to come down?"

"*I* will!" the boy said with extraordinary brightness
l emphasis. He gave me another look charged with that
pression and then marched off alone into church.

15

E BUSINESS WAS PRACTICALLY SETTLED from the moment
ever followed him. It was a pitiful surrender to agita-
n, but my being aware of this had somehow no power to
tore me. I only sat there on my tomb and read into
at my little friend had said to me the fulness of its
aning; by the time I had grasped the whole of which I
l also embraced, for absence, the pretext that I was
amed to offer my pupils and the rest of the congrega-
n such an example of delay. What I said to myself above
was that Miles had got something out of me and that
proof of it, for him, would be just this awkward col-
se. He had got out of me that there was something I
s much afraid of and that he should probably be able
make use of my fear to gain, for his own purpose, more

freedom. My fear was of having to deal with the into
able question of the grounds of his dismissal from scho
for that was really but the question of the horrors gathe
behind. That his uncle should arrive to treat with me
these things was a solution that, strictly speaking, I ou
now to have desired to bring on; but I could so little f
the ugliness and the pain of it that I simply procrastina
and lived from hand to mouth. The boy, to my deep
composure, was immensely in the right, was in a posit
to say to me: "Either you clear up with my guardian
mystery of this interruption of my studies, or you ce
to expect me to lead with you a life that's so unnatural
a boy." What was so unnatural for the particular bo
was concerned with was this sudden revelation of a c
sciousness and a plan.

That was what really overcame me, what prevented
going in. I walked round the church, hesitating, hoveri
I reflected that I had already, with him, hurt myself
yond repair. Therefore I could patch up nothing, an
was too extreme an effort to squeeze beside him i
the pew: he would be so much more sure than ever
pass his arm into mine and make me sit there for an h
in close, silent contact with his commentary on our ta
For the first minute since his arrival I wanted to get av
from him. As I paused beneath the high east window a
listened to the sounds of worship, I was taken with an
pulse that might master me, I felt, completely sho
I give it the least encouragement. I might easily put
end to my predicament by getting away altogether. H
was my chance; there was no one to stop me; I co
give the whole thing up—turn my back and retreat
was only a question of hurrying again, for a few prepa
tions, to the house which the attendance at church o
many of the servants would practically have left
occupied. No one, in short, could blame me if I sho
just drive desperately off. What was it to get away if I
away only till dinner? That would be in a couple of ho
at the end of which—I had the acute prevision—my li

upils would play at innocent wonder about my non-
ppearance in their train.

"What *did* you do, you naughty, bad thing? Why in
he world, to worry us so—and take our thoughts off too,
on't you know?—did you desert us at the very door?" I
ouldn't meet such questions nor, as they asked them,
heir false little lovely eyes; yet it was all so exactly what
should have to meet that, as the prospect grew sharp to
he, I at last let myself go.

I got, so far as the immediate moment was concerned,
way; I came straight out of the churchyard and, think-
ng hard, retraced my steps through the park. It seemed
o me that by the time I reached the house I had made
p my mind I would fly. The Sunday stillness both of the
pproaches and of the interior, in which I met no one,
airly excited me with a sense of opportunity. Were I to
et off quickly, this way, I should get off without a scene,
ithout a word. My quickness would have to be remark-
ble, however, and the question of a conveyance was the
reat one to settle. Tormented, in the hall, with difficul-
es and obstacles, I remember sinking down at the foot
f the staircase—suddenly collapsing there on the lowest
ep and then, with a revulsion, recalling that it was ex-
ctly where more than a month before, in the darkness of
ight and just so bowed with evil things, I had seen the
pectre of the most horrible of women. At this I was able
o straighten myself; I went the rest of the way up; I made,
n my bewilderment, for the schoolroom, where there were
bjects belonging to me that I should have to take. But I
pened the door to find again, in a flash, my eyes unsealed.
n the presence of what I saw I reeled straight back upon
hy resistance.

Seated at my own table in clear noonday light I saw a
erson whom, without my previous experience, I should
ave taken at the first blush for some housemaid who
hight have stayed at home to look after the place and
ho, availing herself of rare relief from observation and
f the schoolroom table and my pens, ink, and paper, had

applied herself to the considerable effort of a letter
her sweetheart. There was an effort in the way that, whi
her arms rested on the table, her hands with evide
weariness supported her head; but at the moment I too
this in I had already become aware that, in spite of n
entrance, her attitude strangely persisted. Then it was
with the very act of its announcing itself—that her ide
tity flared up in a change of posture. She rose, not as
she had heard me, but with an indescribable grand me
ancholy of indifference and detachment, and, within
dozen feet of me, stood there as my vile predecessor. D
honoured and tragic, she was all before me; but even as
fixed and, for memory, secured it, the awful image passe
away. Dark as midnight in her black dress, her hagga
beauty and her unutterable woe, she had looked at n
long enough to appear to say that her right to sit at n
table was as good as mine to sit at hers. While these i
stants lasted indeed I had the extraordinary chill of
feeling that it was I who was the intruder. It was as
wild protest against it that, actually addressing her—"Yc
terrible, miserable woman!"—I heard myself break in
a sound that, by the open door, rang through the lo
passage and the empty house. She looked at me as if sl
heard me, but I had recovered myself and cleared the a
There was nothing in the room the next minute but t
sunshine and a sense that I must stay.

16

I HAD SO PERFECTLY EXPECTED that the return of my pup
would be marked by a demonstration that I was fresh
upset at having to take into account that they were dun
about my absence. Instead of gaily denouncing and care
ing me, they made no allusion to my having failed the
and I was left, for the time, on perceiving that she t
said nothing, to study Mrs. Grose's odd face. I did th

such purpose that I made sure they had in some way
bed her to silence; a silence that, however, I would
gage to break down on the first private opportunity.
his opportunity came before tea: I secured five minutes
th her in the housekeeper's room, where, in the twilight,
id a smell of lately-baked bread, but with the place all
ept and garnished, I found her sitting in pained pla-
ity before the fire. So I see her still, so I see her best:
ing the flame from her straight chair in the dusky,
ning room, a large clean image of the "put away"—of
wers closed and locked and rest without a remedy.

'Oh, yes, they asked me to say nothing; and to please
em—so long as they were there—of course I promised.
t what had happened to you?"

"I only went with you for the walk," I said. "I had then
come back to meet a friend."

She showed her surprise. "A friend—*you?*"

"Oh, yes, I have a couple!" I laughed. "But did the
ildren give you a reason?"

"For not alluding to your leaving us? Yes; they said
u would like it better. Do you like it better?"

My face had made her rueful. "No, I like it worse!" But
er an instant I added: "Did they say why I should like
better?"

"No; Master Miles only said, 'We must do nothing but
at she likes'!"

"I wish indeed he would! And what did Flora say?"

"Miss Flora was too sweet. She said, 'Oh, of course, of
urse!'—and I said the same."

I thought a moment. "You were too sweet too—I can
ar you all. But none the less, between Miles and me,
s now all out."

"All out?" My companion stared. "But what, Miss?"

"Everything. It doesn't matter. I've made up my mind.
ame home, my dear," I went on, "for a talk with Miss
ssel."

I had by this time formed the habit of having Mrs.
ose literally well in hand in advance of my sounding

that note; so that even now, as she bravely blinked ur
the signal of my word, I could keep her comparati
firm. "A talk! Do you mean she spoke?"

"It came to that. I found her, on my return, in
schoolroom."

"And what did she say?" I can hear the good wo₁
still, and the candour of her stupefaction.

"That she suffers the torments—!"

It was this, of a truth, that made her, as she filled
my picture, gape. "Do you mean," she faltered, "—of
lost?"

"Of the lost. Of the damned. And that's why, to sl
them—" I faltered myself with the horror of it.

But my companion, with less imagination, kept me
"To share them—?"

"She wants Flora." Mrs. Grose might, as I gave i
her, fairly have fallen away from me had I not been
pared. I still held her there, to show I was. "As I've
you, however, it doesn't matter."

"Because you've made up your mind? But to what?'

"To everything."

"And what do you call 'everything'?"

"Why, sending for their uncle."

"Oh, Miss, in pity do," my friend broke out.

"Ah, but I will, I *will*! I see it's the only way. Wl
'out,' as I told you, with Miles is that if he thinks
afraid to—and has ideas of what he gains by that
shall see he's mistaken. Yes, yes; his uncle shall hav
here from me on the spot (and before the boy himse
necessary) that if I'm to be reproached with having c
nothing again about more school—"

"Yes, Miss—" my companion pressed me.

"Well, there's that awful reason."

There were now clearly so many of these for my ₁
colleague that she was excusable for being vague.
—a—which?"

"Why, the letter from his old place."

"You'll show it to the master?"

"I ought to have done so on the instant."

"Oh, no!" said Mrs. Grose with decision.

"I'll put it before him," I went on inexorably, "that I can't undertake to work the question on behalf of a child who has been expelled—"

"For we've never in the least known what!" Mrs. Grose declared.

"For wickedness. For what else—when he's so clever and beautiful and perfect? Is he stupid? Is he untidy? Is he infirm? Is he ill-natured? He's exquisite—so it can be only *that;* and that would open up the whole thing. After all," I said, "it's their uncle's fault. If he left here such people—!"

"He didn't really in the least know them. The fault's mine." She had turned quite pale.

"Well, you shan't suffer," I answered.

I was silent awhile; we looked at each other. "Then what am I to tell him?"

"You needn't tell him anything. *I'll* tell him."

I measured this. "Do you mean you'll write—?" Remembering she couldn't, I caught myself up. "How do you communicate?"

"I tell the bailiff. *He* writes."

"And should you like him to write our story?"

My question had a sarcastic force that I had not fully intended, and it made her, after a moment, inconsequently break down. The tears were again in her eyes. "Ah, Miss, *you* write!"

"Well—tonight," I at last answered; and on this we separated.

I WENT SO FAR, in the evening, as to make a beginning. The weather had changed back, a great wind was abroad, and beneath the lamp, in my room, with Flora at peace

beside me, I sat for a long time before a blank sheet of
paper and listened to the lash of the rain and the batter
of the gusts. Finally I went out, taking a candle; I crossed
the passage and listened a minute at Miles's door. What,
under my endless obsession, I had been impelled to listen
for was some betrayal of his not being at rest, and I presently caught one, but not in the form I had expected. His
voice tinkled out. "I say, you there—come in." It was a
gaiety in the gloom!

I went in with my light and found him, in bed, very
wide awake, but very much at his ease. "Well, what are
you up to?" he asked with a grace of sociability in which
it occurred to me that Mrs. Grose, had she been present,
might have looked in vain for proof that anything was
"out."

I stood over him with my candle. "How did you know
I was there?"

"Why, of course I heard you. Did you fancy you made
no noise? You're like a troop of cavalry!" he beautifully
laughed.

"Then you weren't asleep?"

"Not much! I lie awake and think."

I had put my candle, designedly, a short way off, and
then, as he held out his friendly old hand to me, had sat
down on the edge of his bed. "What is it," I asked, "that
you think of?"

"What in the world, my dear, but *you?*"

"Ah, the pride I take in your appreciation doesn't insist
on that! I had so far rather you slept."

"Well, I think also, you know, of this queer business of
ours."

I marked the coolness of his firm little hand. "Of what
queer business, Miles?"

"Why, the way you bring me up. And all the rest!"

I fairly held my breath a minute, and even from my
glimmering taper there was light enough to show how
he smiled up at me from his pillow. "What do you mean
by all the rest?"

"Oh, you know, you know!"

I could say nothing for a minute, though I felt, as I held his hand and our eyes continued to meet, that my silence had all the air of admitting his charge and that nothing in the whole world of reality was perhaps at that moment so fabulous as our actual relation. "Certainly you shall go back to school," I said, "if it be that that troubles you. But not to the old place—we must find another, a better. How could I know it did trouble you, this question, when you never told me so, never spoke of it at all?" His clear, listening face, framed in its smooth whiteness, made him for the minute as appealing as some wistful patient in children's hospital; and I would have given, as the resemblance came to me, all I possessed on earth really to be the nurse or the sister of charity who might have helped to cure him. Well, even as it was, I perhaps might help! Do you know you've never said a word to me about your school—I mean the old one; never mentioned it in any way?"

He seemed to wonder; he smiled with the same loveliness. But he clearly gained time; he waited, he called for guidance. "Haven't I?" It wasn't for *me* to help him—it was for the thing I had met!

Something in his tone and the expression of his face, as I got this from him, set my heart aching with such a pang as it had never yet known; so unutterably touching was it to see his little brain puzzled and his little resources taxed to play, under the spell laid on him, a part of innocence and consistency. "No, never—from the hour you came back. You've never mentioned to me one of your masters, one of your comrades, nor the least little thing that ever happened to you at school. Never, little Miles—no, never—have you given me an inkling of anything that may have happened there. Therefore you can fancy how much I'm in the dark. Until you came out, that way, this morning, you had, since the first hour I saw you, scarce even made a reference to anything in your previous life. You seemed so perfectly to accept the present." It was

extraordinary how my absolute conviction of his secre
precocity (or whatever I might call the poison of an in
fluence that I dared but half to phrase) made him, in spit
of the faint breath of his inward trouble, appear as ac
cessible as an older person—imposed him almost as a
intellectual equal. "I thought you wanted to go on a
you are."

It struck me that at this he just faintly coloured. H
gave, at any rate, like a convalescent slightly fatigued,
languid shake of his head. "I don't—I don't. I want to g
away."

"You're tired of Bly?"

"Oh, no, I like Bly."

"Well, then—?"

"Oh, *you* know what a boy wants!"

I felt that I didn't know as well as Miles, and I too
temporary refuge. "You want to go to your uncle?"

Again, at this, with his sweet ironic face, he made
movement on the pillow. "Ah, you can't get off wit
that!"

I was silent a little, and it was I, now, I think, wh
changed colour. "My dear, I don't want to get off!"

"You can't, even if you do. You can't, you can't!"—h
lay beautifully staring. "My uncle must come down, an
you must completely settle things."

"If we do," I returned with some spirit, "you may b
sure it will be to take you quite away."

"Well, don't you understand that that's exactly wha
I'm working for? You'll have to tell him—about the wa
you've let it all drop: you'll have to tell him a tremendou
lot!"

The exultation with which he uttered this helped m
somehow, for the instant, to meet him rather more. "An
how much will *you*, Miles, have to tell him? There ar
things he'll ask you!"

He turned it over. "Very likely. But what things?"

"The things you've never told me. To make up h
mind what to do with you. He can't send you back—"

"Oh, I don't want to go back!" he broke in. "I want a new field."

He said it with admirable serenity, with positive unimpeachable gaiety; and doubtless it was that very note that most evoked for me the poignancy, the unnatural childish tragedy, of his probable reappearance at the end of three months with all this bravado and still more dishonour. It overwhelmed me now that I should never be able to bear that, and it made me let myself go. I threw myself upon him and in the tenderness of my pity I embraced him. "Dear little Miles, dear little Miles—!"

My face was close to his, and he let me kiss him, simply taking it with indulgent good-humour. "Well, old lady?"

"Is there nothing—nothing at all that you want to tell me?"

He turned off a little, facing round toward the wall and holding up his hand to look at as one had seen sick children look. "I've told you—I told you this morning."

Oh, I was sorry for him! "That you just want me not to worry you?"

He looked round at me now, as if in recognition of my understanding him; then ever so gently, "To let me alone," he replied.

There was even a singular little dignity in it, something that made me release him, yet, when I had slowly risen, linger beside him. God knows I never wished to harass him, but I felt that merely, at this, to turn my back on him was to abandon or, to put it more truly, to lose him. "I've just begun a letter to your uncle," I said.

"Well, then, finish it!"

I waited a minute. "What happened before?"

He gazed up at me again. "Before what?"

"Before you came back. And before you went away."

For some time he was silent, but he continued to meet my eyes. "What happened?"

It made me, the sound of the words, in which it seemed to me that I caught for the very first time a small faint quaver of consenting consciousness—it made me drop on my knees beside the bed and seize once more the chance of possessing him. "Dear little Miles, dear little Miles, if you *knew* how I want to help you! It's only that, it's nothing but that, and I'd rather die than give you a pain or do you a wrong—I'd rather die than hurt a hair of you. Dear little Miles"—oh, I brought it out now even if I *should* go too far—"I just want you to help me to save you!" But I knew in a moment after this that I had gone too far. The answer to my appeal was instantaneous, but it came in the form of an extraordinary blast and chill, a gust of frozen air and a shake of the room as great as if, in the wild wind, the casement had crashed in. The boy gave a loud, high shriek, which, lost in the rest of the shock of sound, might have seemed, indistinctly, though I was so close to him, a note either of jubilation or of terror. I jumped to my feet again and was conscious of darkness. So for a moment we remained, while I stared about me and saw that the drawn curtains were unstirred and the window tight. "Why, the candle's out!" I then cried.

"It was I who blew it, dear!" said Miles.

THE NEXT DAY, after lessons, Mrs. Grose found a moment to say to me quietly: "Have you written, Miss?"

"Yes—I've written." But I didn't add—for the hour—that my letter, sealed and directed, was still in my pocket. There would be time enough to send it before the messenger should go to the village. Meanwhile there had been, on the part of my pupils, no more brilliant, more exemplary morning. It was exactly as if they had both had at heart to gloss over any recent little friction. They performed the dizziest feats of arithmetic, soaring quite out of *my* feeble range, and perpetrated, in higher spirits than ever, geographical and historical jokes. It was conspicuous of course in Miles in particular that he appeared

wish to show how easily he could let me down. This
ild, to my memory, really lives in a setting of beauty
d misery that no words can translate; there was a dis-
ction all his own in every impulse he revealed; never
s a small natural creature, to the uninitiated eye all
inkness and freedom, a more ingenious, a more ex-
aordinary little gentleman. I had perpetually to guard
ainst the wonder of contemplation into which my in-
ated view betrayed me; to check the irrelevant gaze
d discouraged sigh in which I constantly both attacked
d renounced the enigma of what such a little gentle-
an could have done that deserved a penalty. Say that, by
e dark prodigy I knew, the imagination of all evil *had*
en opened up to him: all the justice within me ached
r the proof that it could ever have flowered into an act.

He had never, at any rate, been such a little gentleman
when, after our early dinner on this dreadful day, he
me round to me and asked if I shouldn't like him, for
lf an hour, to play to me. David playing to Saul could
ver have shown a finer sense of the occasion. It was
erally a charming exhibition of tact, of magnanimity,
d quite tantamount to his saying outright: "The true
ights we love to read about never push an advantage
o far. I know what you mean now: you mean that—
be let alone yourself and not followed up—you'll cease
worry and spy upon me, won't keep me so close to you,
ll let me go and come. Well, I 'come,' you see—but I
n't go! There'll be plenty of time for that. I do really
light in your society, and I only want to show you that
contended for a principle." It may be imagined whether
resisted this appeal or failed to accompany him again,
nd in hand, to the schoolroom. He sat down at the old
ano and played as he had never played, and if there are
ose who think he had better have been kicking a foot-
ll I can only say that I wholly agree with them. For at
e end of a time that under his influence I had quite
ased to measure I started up with a strange sense of hav-
g literally slept at my post. It was after luncheon, and

by the schoolroom fire, and yet I hadn't really, in the lea
slept: I had only done something much worse—I had fo
gotten. Where, all this time, was Flora? When I put t
question to Miles he played on a minute before a
swering, and then could only say: "Why, my dear, ho
do I know?"—breaking moreover into a happy laug
which, immediately after, as if it were a vocal accompan
ment, he prolonged into incoherent, extravagant song.

I went straight to my room, but his sister was not ther
then, before going downstairs, I looked into several othe
As she was nowhere about she would surely be with M
Grose, whom, in the comfort of that theory, I according
proceeded in quest of. I found her where I had found h
the evening before, but she met my quick challenge wi
blank, scared ignorance. She had only supposed that, aft
the repast, I had carried off both the children; as to whi
she was quite in her right, for it was the very first tin
I had allowed the little girl out of my sight without sor
special provision. Of course now indeed she might be wi
the maids, so that the immediate thing was to look f
her without an air of alarm. This we promptly arrang
between us; but when, ten minutes later and in pursuan
of our arrangement, we met in the hall, it was only
report on either side that after guarded inquiries we ha
altogether failed to trace her. For a minute there, apa
from observation, we exchanged mute alarms, and I cou
feel with what high interest my friend returned me a
those I had from the first given her.

"She'll be above," she presently said—"in one of t
rooms you haven't searched."

"No; she's at a distance." I had made up my mind. "S
has gone out."

Mrs. Grose stared. "Without a hat?"

I naturally also looked volumes. "Isn't that woma
always without one?"

"She's with *her?*"

"She's with *her!*" I declared. "We must find them."

My hand was on my friend's arm, but she failed for t

moment, confronted with such an account of the matter,
to respond to my pressure. She communed, on the contrary, on the spot, with her uneasiness. "And where's
Master Miles?"

"Oh, *he's* with Quint. They're in the schoolroom."

"Lord, Miss!" My view, I was myself aware—and therefore I suppose my tone—had never yet reached so calm
an assurance.

"The trick's played," I went on; "they've successfully
worked their plan. He found the most divine little way to
keep me quiet while she went off."

" 'Divine'?" Mrs. Grose bewilderedly echoed.

"Infernal, then!" I almost cheerfully rejoined. "He has
provided for himself as well. But come!"

She had helplessly gloomed at the upper regions. "You
leave him—?"

"So long with Quint? Yes—I don't mind that now."

She always ended, at these moments, by getting possession of my hand, and in this manner she could at present
still stay me. But after gasping an instant at my sudden
resignation, "Because of your letter?" she eagerly brought
out.

I quickly, by way of answer, felt for my letter, drew it
forth, held it up, and then, freeing myself, went and laid
on the great hall-table. "Luke will take it," I said as I
came back. I reached the house-door and opened it; I was
already on the steps.

My companion still demurred: the storm of the night
and the early morning had dropped, but the afternoon
was damp and grey. I came down to the drive while she
stood in the doorway. "You go with nothing on?"

"What do I care when the child has nothing? I can't
wait to dress," I cried, "and if you must do so, I leave you.
Try meanwhile, yourself, upstairs."

"With *them*?" Oh, on this, the poor woman promptly
joined me!

19

WE WENT STRAIGHT TO THE LAKE, as it was called at Bly, an
I dare say rightly called, though I reflect that it may in
fact have been a sheet of water less remarkable than
appeared to my untravelled eyes. My acquaintance wi
sheets of water was small, and the pool of Bly, at a
events on the few occasions of my consenting, under t
protection of my pupils, to affront its surface in the o
flat-bottomed boat moored there for our use, had in
pressed me both with its extent and its agitation. T
usual place of embarkation was half a mile from t
house, but I had an intimate conviction that, wherev
Flora might be, she was not near home. She had not giv
me the slip for any small adventure, and, since the day
the very great one that I had shared with her by the pon
I had been aware, in our walks, of the quarter to whi
she most inclined. This was why I had now given to M
Grose's steps so marked a direction—a direction that ma
her, when she perceived it, oppose a resistance that show
me she was freshly mystified. "You're going to the wate
Miss?—you think she's in—?"

"She may be, though the depth is, I believe, nowhe
very great. But what I judge most likely is that she's a
the spot from which, the other day, we saw together wh
I told you."

"When she pretended not to see—?"

"With that astounding self-possession! I've always be
sure she wanted to go back alone. And now her broth
has managed it for her."

Mrs. Grose still stood where she had stopped. "You su
pose they really *talk* of them?"

I could meet this with a confidence! "They say thin
that, if we heard them, would simply appall us."

"And if she *is* there—?"

"Yes?"

"Then Miss Jessel is?"

"Beyond a doubt. You shall see."

"Oh, thank you!" my friend cried, planted so firm that, taking it in, I went straight on without her. By the time I reached the pool, however, she was close behind me, and I knew that, whatever, to her apprehension, might befall me, the exposure of my society struck her as her least danger. She exhaled a moan of relief as we at last came in sight of the greater part of the water without a sight of the child. There was no trace of Flora on that nearer side of the bank where my observation of her had been most startling, and none on the opposite edge, where, save for a margin of some twenty yards, a thick copse came down to the water. The pond, oblong in shape, had a width so scant compared to its length that, with its ends out of view, it might have been taken for a scant river. We looked at the empty expanse, and then I felt the suggestion of my friend's eyes. I knew what she meant and I replied with a negative headshake.

"No, no; wait! She has taken the boat."

My companion stared at the vacant mooring-place and then again across the lake. "Then where is it?"

"Our not seeing it is the strongest of proofs. She has used it to go over, and then has managed to hide it."

"All alone—that child?"

"She's not alone, and at such times she's not a child: she's an old, old woman." I scanned all the visible shore while Mrs. Grose took again, into the queer element I offered her, one of her plunges of submission; then I pointed out that the boat might perfectly be in a small refuge formed by one of the recesses of the pool, an indentation masked, for the hither side, by a projection of the bank and by a clump of trees growing close to the water.

"But if the boat's there, where on earth's *she?*" my colleague anxiously asked.

"That's exactly what we must learn." And I started to

walk further.

"By going all the way round?"

"Certainly, far as it is. It will take us but ten minutes, but it's far enough to have made the child prefer not to walk. She went straight over."

"Laws!" cried my friend again; the chain of my logic was ever too much for her. It dragged her at my heels even now, and when we had got half-way round—a devious tiresome process, on ground much broken and by a path choked with overgrowth—I paused to give her breath. sustained her with a grateful arm, assuring her that she might hugely help me; and this started us afresh, so that in the course of but a few minutes more we reached a point from which we found the boat to be where I had supposed it. It had been intentionally left as much as possible out of sight and was tied to one of the stakes of a fence that came, just there, down to the brink and that had been an assistance to disembarking. I recognised, as I looked at the pair of short, thick oars, quite safely drawn up, the prodigious character of the feat for a little girl but I had lived, by this time, too long among wonders and had panted to too many livelier measures. There was a gate in the fence, through which we passed, and that brought us, after a trifling interval, more into the open. Then, "There she is!" we both exclaimed at once.

Flora, a short way off, stood before us on the grass and smiled as if her performance was now complete. The next thing she did, however, was to stoop straight down and pluck—quite as if it were all she was there for—a big ugly spray of withered fern. I instantly became sure she had just come out of the copse. She waited for us, not herself taking a step, and I was conscious of the rare solemnity with which we presently approached her. She smiled and smiled, and we met; but it was all done in silence by this time flagrantly ominous. Mrs. Grose was the first to break the spell: she threw herself on her knees and, drawing the child to her breast, clasped in a long embrace the little tender, yielding body. While the

umb convulsion lasted I could only watch it—which I
d the more intently when I saw Flora's face peep at me
er our companion's shoulder. It was serious now—the
cker had left it; but it strengthened the pang with which
at that moment envied Mrs. Grose the simplicity of *her*
lation. Still, all this while, nothing more passed be-
een us save that Flora had let her foolish fern again
op to the ground. What she and I had virtually said to
ch other was that pretexts were useless now. When
rs. Grose finally got up she kept the child's hand, so
at the two were still before me; and the singular reti-
nce of our communion was even more marked in the
ank look she launched me. "I'll be hanged," it said, "if
l speak!"

It was Flora who, gazing all over me in candid wonder,
us the first. She was struck with our bareheaded aspect.
Vhy, where are your things?"

"Where yours are, my dear!" I promptly returned.

She had already got back her gaiety, and appeared to
ke this as an answer quite sufficient. "And where's
iles?" she went on.

There was something in the small valour of it that
ite finished me: these three words from her were, in a
sh like the glitter of a drawn blade, the jostle of the
p that my hand, for weeks and weeks, had held high
d full to the brim and that now, even before speaking,
felt overflow in a deluge. "I'll tell you if you'll tell
e—" I heard myself say, then heard the tremor in which
broke.

"Well, what?"

Mrs. Grose's suspense blazed at me, but it was too late
w, and I brought the thing out handsomely. "Where,
/ pet, is Miss Jessel?"

20

JUST AS IN THE CHURCHYARD WITH MILES, the whole thi
was upon us. Much as I had made of the fact that th
name had never once, between us, been sounded, t
quick, smitten glare with which the child's face now
ceived it fairly likened my breach of the silence to t
smash of a pane of glass. It added to the interposing c
as if to stay the blow, that Mrs. Grose, at the same insta
uttered over my violence—the shriek of a creature scare
or rather wounded, which, in turn, within a few secon
was completed by a gasp of my own. I seized my c
league's arm. "She's there, she's there!"

Miss Jessel stood before us on the opposite bank exac
as she had stood the other time, and I rememb
strangely, as the first feeling now produced in me,
thrill of joy at having brought on a proof. She was the
and I was justified; she was there, and I was neither cru
nor mad. She was there for poor scared Mrs. Grose, b
she was there most for Flora; and no moment of my mo
strous time was perhaps so extraordinary as that in whi
I consciously threw out to her—with the sense that, pa
and ravenous demon as she was, she would catch a
understand it—an inarticulate message of gratitude. S
rose erect on the spot my friend and I had lately quitte
and there was not, in all the long reach of her desire,
inch of her evil that fell short. This first vividness
vision and emotion were things of a few seconds, duri
which Mrs. Grose's dazed blink across to where I point
struck me as a sovereign sign that she too at last saw, j
as it carried my own eyes precipitately to the child. T
revelation then of the manner in which Flora was affect
startled me, in truth, far more than it would have done
find her also merely agitated, for direct dismay was
course not what I had expected. Prepared and on h
guard as our pursuit had actually made her, she wou

epress every betrayal; and I was therefore shaken, on the
pot, by my first glimpse of the particular one for which
had not allowed. To see her, without a convulsion of
er small pink face, not even feign to glance in the direc-
ion of the prodigy I announced, but only, instead of
hat, turn at *me* an expression of hard, still gravity, an
xpression absolutely new and unprecedented and that
ppeared to read and accuse and judge me—this was a
:roke that somehow converted the little girl herself into
1e very presence that could make me quail. I quailed
ven though my certitude that she thoroughly saw was
ever greater than at that instant, and in the immediate
eed to defend myself I called it passionately to witness.
She's there, you little unhappy thing—there, there, *there,*
nd you see her as well as you see me!" I had said shortly
efore to Mrs. Grose that she was not at these times a
hild, but an old, old woman, and that description of
er could not have been more strikingly confirmed than
1 the way in which, for all answer to this, she simply
1owed me, without a concession, an admission, of her
yes, a countenance of deeper and deeper, of indeed sud-
enly quite fixed, reprobation. I was by this time—if I
1n put the whole thing at all together—more appalled
t what I may properly call her manner than at anything
lse, though it was simultaneously with this that I be-
ame aware of having Mrs. Grose also, and very formid-
bly, to reckon with. My elder companion, the next mo-
1ent, at any rate, blotted out everything but her own
ushed face and her loud, shocked protest, a burst of high
isapproval. "What a dreadful turn, to be sure, Miss!
Vhere on earth do you see anything?"

I could only grasp her more quickly yet, for even while
1e spoke the hideous plain presence stood undimmed
nd undaunted. It had already lasted a minute, and it
isted while I continued, seizing my colleague, quite
1rusting her at it and presenting her to it, to insist with
1y pointing hand. "You don't see her exactly as *we* see?
you mean to say you don't now—*now?* She's as big as

a blazing fire! Only look, dearest woman, *look—!*" She
looked, even as I did, and gave me, with her deep groan
of negation, repulsion, compassion—the mixture with her
pity of her relief at her exemption—a sense, touching to
me even then, that she would have backed me up if she
could. I might well have needed that, for with this hard
blow of the proof that her eyes were hopelessly sealed I
felt my own situation horribly crumble, I felt—I saw—
my livid predecessor press, from her position, on my defeat, and I was conscious, more than all, of what I should
have from this instant to deal with in the astounding little
attitude of Flora. Into this attitude Mrs. Grose immediately and violently entered, breaking, even while there
pierced through my sense of ruin a prodigious private
triumph, into breathless reassurance.

"She isn't there, little lady, and nobody's there—and you
never see nothing, my sweet! How can poor Miss Jessel—
when poor Miss Jessel's dead and buried? *We* know,
don't we, love?"—and she appealed, blundering in, to the
child. "It's all a mere mistake and a worry and a joke—
and we'll go home as fast as we can!"

Our companion, on this, had responded with a strange
quick primness of propriety, and they were again, with
Mrs. Grose on her feet, united, as it were, in pained opposition to me. Flora continued to fix me with her small
mask of reprobation, and even at that minute I prayed
God to forgive me for seeming to see that, as she stood
there holding tight to our friend's dress, her incomparable
childish beauty had suddenly failed, had quite vanished.
I've said it already—she was literally, she was hideously
hard; she had turned common and almost ugly. "I don't
know what you mean. I see nobody. I see nothing. I never
·*have*. I think you're cruel. I don't like you!" Then, after
this deliverance, which might have been that of a vulgarly
pert little girl in the street, she hugged Mrs. Grose more
closely and buried in her skirts the dreadful little face.
In this position she produced an almost furious wail.
"Take me away, take me away—oh, take me away from

!"

From *me?*" I panted.

From you—from you!" she cried.

ven Mrs. Grose looked across at me dismayed, while
ad nothing to do but communicate again with the
re that, on the opposite bank, without a movement,
rigidly still as if catching, beyond the interval, our
ces, was as vividly there for my disaster as it was not
re for my service. The wretched child had spoken
ctly as if she had got from some outside source each
her stabbing little words, and I could therefore, in the
despair of all I had to accept, but sadly shake my head
her. "If I had ever doubted, all my doubt would at
sent have gone. I've been living with the miserable
th, and now it has only too much closed round me. Of
rse I've lost you: I've interfered, and you've seen
nder her dictation"—with which I faced, over the
l again, our infernal witness—"the easy and perfect
 to meet it. I've done my best, but I've lost you. Good-
." For Mrs. Grose I had an imperative, an almost fran-
'Go, go!" before which, in infinite distress, but mutely
sessed of the little girl and clearly convinced, in spite of
blindness, that something awful had occurred and
e collapse engulfed us, she retreated, by the way we
come, as fast as she could move.

f what first happened when I was left alone I had no
sequent memory. I only knew that at the end of, I
pose, a quarter of an hour, an odorous dampness and
ghness, chilling and piercing my trouble, had made
understand that I must have thrown myself, on my
, on the ground and given way to a wildness of grief.
ust have lain there long and cried and sobbed, for
n I raised my head the day was almost done. I got up
looked a moment, through the twilight, at the grey
l and its blank, haunted edge, and then I took, back
the house, my dreary and difficult course. When
ached the gate in the fence the boat, to my surprise,
gone, so that I had a fresh reflection to make on

Flora's extraordinary command of the situation. S
passed that night, by the most tacit, and I should ad
were not the word so grotesque a false note, the happi
of arrangements, with Mrs. Grose. I saw neither of th
on my return, but, on the other hand as by an ambiguc
compensation, I saw a great deal of Miles. I saw—I c
use no other phrase—so much of him that it was as if
were more than it had ever been. No evening I had pass
at Bly had the portentous quality of this one; in spite
which—and in spite also of the deeper depths of const
nation that had opened beneath my feet—there was lit
ally, in the ebbing actual, an extraordinarily sweet s
ness. On reaching the house I had never so much as look
for the boy; I had simply gone straight to my room
change what I was wearing and to take in, at a glan
much material testimony to Flora's rupture. Her little
longings had all been removed. When later, by the scho
room fire, I was served with tea by the usual maid, I
dulged, on the article of my other pupil, in no inqu
whatever. He had his freedom now—he might have it
the end! Well, he did have it; and it consisted—in part
least—of his coming in at about eight o'clock and sitt
down with me in silence. On the removal of the tea-thir
I had blown out the candles and drawn my chair clos
I was conscious of a mortal coldness and felt as if I sho
never again be warm. So, when he appeared, I was sitt
in the glow with my thoughts. He paused a moment
the door as if to look at me; then—as if to share ther
came to the other side of the hearth and sank into a cha
We sat there in absolute stillness; yet he wanted, I felt,
be with me.

BEFORE A NEW DAY, in my room, had fully broken,
eyes opened to Mrs. Grose, who had come to my beds

ith worse news. Flora was so markedly feverish that an
lness was perhaps at hand; she had passed a night of
xtreme unrest, a night agitated above all by fears that
ad for their subject not in the least her former, but
holly her present, governess. It was not against the
ossible re-entrance of Miss Jessel on the scene that she
rotested—it was conspicuously and passionately against
ine. I was promptly on my feet of course, and with an
nmense deal to ask; the more that my friend had dis-
rnibly now girded her loins to meet me once more.
his I felt as soon as I had put to her the question of her
nse of the child's sincerity as against my own. "She per-
sts in denying to you that she saw, or has ever seen,
ything?"

My visitor's trouble, truly, was great. "Ah, Miss, it isn't
matter on which I can push her! Yet it isn't either, I
ust say, as if I much needed to. It has made her, every
ch of her, quite old."

"Oh, I see her perfectly from here. She resents, for all
e world like some high little personage, the imputation
1 her truthfulness and, as it were, her respectability.
liss Jessel indeed—*she!*' Ah, she's 'respectable,' the chit!
he impression she gave me there yesterday was, I assure
ou, the very strangest of all; it was quite beyond any of
the others. I *did* put my foot in it! She'll never speak
me again."

Hideous and obscure as it all was, it held Mrs. Grose
riefly silent; then she granted my point with a frank-
ss which, I made sure, had more behind it. "I think in-
ed, Miss, she never will. She do have a grand manner
)out it!"

"And that manner"—I summed it up—"is practically
hat's the matter with her now!"

Oh, that manner, I could see in my visitor's face, and
)t a little else besides! "She asks me every three minutes
I think you're coming in."

"I see—I see." I too, on my side, had so much more
an worked it out. "Has she said to you since yesterday

107

—except to repudiate her familiarity with anything s
dreadful—a single other word about Miss Jessel?"

"Not one, Miss. And of course you know," my frien
added, "I took it from her, by the lake, that, just the
and there at least, there *was* nobody."

"Rather! And, naturally, you take it from her still."

"I don't contradict her. What else can I do?"

"Nothing in the world! You've the cleverest little pe
son to deal with. They've made them—their two friend
I mean—still cleverer even than nature did; for it wa
wondrous material to play on! Flora has now her grie
ance, and she'll work it to the end."

"Yes, Miss; but to *what* end?"

"Why, that of dealing with me to her uncle. She'
make me out to him the lowest creature—!"

I winced at the fair show of the scene in Mrs. Gros
face; she looked for a minute as if she sharply saw the
together. "And him who thinks so well of you!"

"He has an odd way—it comes over me now," I laughe
"—of proving it! But that doesn't matter. What Flor
wants, of course, is to get rid of me."

My companion bravely concurred. "Never again to s
much as look at you."

"So that what you've come to me now for," I aske
"is to speed me on my way?" Before she had time to repl
however, I had her in check. "I've a better idea—the resu
of my reflections. My going *would* seem the right thin
and on Sunday I was terribly near it. Yet that won't d
It's *you* who must go. You must take Flora."

My visitor, at this, did speculate. "But where in th
world—?"

"Away from here. Away from *them*. Away, even mo
of all, now, from me. Straight to her uncle."

"Only to tell on you—?"

"No, not 'only'! To leave me, in addition, with n
remedy."

She was still vague. "And what *is* your remedy?"

"Your loyalty, to begin with. And then Miles's."

She looked at me hard. "Do you think he—?"

"Won't if he has the chance, turn on me? Yes, I venture
ll to think it. At all events, I want to try. Get off with
 sister as soon as possible and leave me with him alone."

vas amazed, myself, at the spirit I had still in reserve,
d therefore perhaps a trifle the more disconcerted at
e way in which, in spite of this fine example of it, she
sitated. "There's one thing, of course," I went on: "they
istn't, before she goes, see each other for three seconds."
Then it came over me that, in spite of Flora's presum-
le sequestration from the instant of her return from the
ol, it might already be too late. "Do you mean," I
xiously asked, "that they *have* met?"

At this she quite flushed. "Ah, Miss, I'm not such a
ol as that! If I've been obliged to leave her three or four
nes, it has been each time with one of the maids, and
 present, though she's alone, she's locked in safe. And
—and yet!" There were too many things.

"And yet what?"

"Well, are you so sure of the little gentleman?"

"I'm not sure of anything but *you*. But I have, since
t evening, a new hope. I think he wants to give me an
ening. I do believe that—poor little exquisite wretch!
ie wants to speak. Last evening, in the firelight and the
ence, he sat with me for two hours as if it were just
ning."

Mrs. Grose looked hard, through the window, at the
y, gathering day. "And did it come?"

"No, though I waited and waited, I confess it didn't,
d it was without a breach of the silence or so much as
aint allusion to his sister's condition and absence that
 at last kissed for good-night. All the same," I con-
ued, "I can't, if her uncle sees her, consent to his seeing
 brother without my having given the boy—and most
all because things have got so bad—a little more time."

My friend appeared on this ground more reluctant than
ould quite understand. "What do you mean by more
ie?"

"Well, a day or two—really to bring it out. He'll th
be on *my* side—of which you see the importance. If no
ing comes, I shall only fail, and you will, at the wor
have helped me by doing, on your arrival in town, wh
ever you may have found possible." So I put it before h
but she continued for a little so inscrutably embarras
that I came again to her aid. "Unless, indeed," I wou
up, "you really want *not* to go."

I could see it, in her face, at last clear itself; she p
out her hand to me as a pledge. "I'll go—I'll go. I'll go t
morning."

I wanted to be very just. "If you *should* wish still
wait, I would engage she shouldn't see me."

"No, no: it's the place itself. She must leave it." S
held me a moment with heavy eyes, then brought out
rest. "Your idea's the right one. I myself, Miss—"

"Well?"

"I can't stay."

The look she gave me with it made me jump at p
sibilities. "You mean that, since yesterday, you h
seen—?"

She shook her head with dignity. "I've *heard*—!"

"Heard?"

"From that child—horrors! There!" she sighed w
tragic relief. "On my honour, Miss, she says things—
But at this evocation she broke down; she dropped, w
a sudden sob, upon my sofa and, as I had seen her do
fore, gave way to all the grief of it.

It was quite in another manner that I, for my part,
myself go. "Oh, thank God!"

She sprang up again at this, drying her eyes with
groan. " 'Thank God'?"

"It so justifies me!"

"It does that, Miss!"

I couldn't have desired more emphasis, but I just h
tated. "She's so horrible?"

I saw my colleague scarce knew how to put it. "Rea
shocking."

"And about me?"

"About you, Miss—since you must have it. It's beyond everything, for a young lady; and I can't think wherever he must have picked up—"

"The appalling language she applied to me? I can, then!" I broke in with a laugh that was doubtless significant enough.

It only, in truth, left my friend still more grave. "Well, perhaps I ought to also—since I've heard some of it before! Yet I can't bear it," the poor woman went on while, with the same movement, she glanced, on my dressing-table, at the face of my watch. "But I must go back."

I kept her, however. "Ah, if you can't bear it—!"

"How can I stop with her, you mean? Why, just *for* that: to get her away. Far from this," she pursued, "far from *them*—"

"She may be different? she may be free?" I seized her almost with joy. "Then, in spite of yesterday, you *believe*—"

"In such doings?" Her simple description of them required, in the light of her expression, to be carried no further, and she gave me the whole thing as she had never done. "I believe."

Yes, it was a joy, and we were still shoulder to shoulder: I might continue sure of that I should care but little what else happened. My support in the presence of disaster would be the same as it had been in my early need of confidence, and if my friend would answer for my honesty, I would answer for all the rest. On the point of taking leave of her, none the less, I was to some extent embarrassed. "There's one thing of course—it occurs to me to remember. My letter, giving the alarm, will have reached town before you."

I now perceived still more how she had been beating about the bush and how weary at last it had made her. "Your letter won't have got there. Your letter never went."

"What then became of it?"

"Goodness knows! Master Miles—"

"Do you mean *he* took it?" I gasped.

She hung fire, but she overcame her reluctance. "I mea
that I saw yesterday, when I came back with Miss Flor
that it wasn't where you had put it. Later in the eveni
I had the chance to question Luke, and he declared th
he had neither noticed nor touched it." We could on
exchange, on this, one of our deeper mutual sounding
and it was Mrs. Grose who first brought up the plun
with an almost elate "You see!"

"Yes, I see that if Miles took it instead he probably w
have read it and destroyed it."

"And don't you see anything else?"

I faced her a moment with a sad smile. "It strikes n
that by this time your eyes are open even wider th
mine."

They proved to be so indeed, but she could still blus
almost, to show it. "I make out now what he must ha
done at school." And she gave, in her simple sharpne
an almost droll disillusioned nod. "He stole!"

I turned it over—I tried to be more judicial. "Well
perhaps."

She looked as if she found me unexpectedly calm. "F
stole *letters!*"

She couldn't know my reasons for a calmness after a
pretty shallow; so I showed them off as I might. "I ho
then it was to more purpose than in this case! The no
at any rate, that I put on the table yesterday," I pursue
"will have given him so scant an advantage—for it co
tained only the bare demand for an interview—that he
already much ashamed of having gone so far for so litt
and that what he had on his mind last evening was pr
cisely the need of confession." I seemed to myself, f
the instant, to have mastered it, to see it all. "Leave t
leave us"—I was already, at the door, hurrying her o
"I'll get it out of him. He'll meet me—he'll confess. If
confesses, he's saved. And if he's saved—"

"Then *you* are?" The dear woman kissed me on th

112

nd I took her farewell. "I'll save you without him!" she
ried as she went.

22

ET IT WAS WHEN SHE HAD GOT OFF—and I missed her on
he spot—that the great pinch really came. If I had counted
n what it would give me to find myself alone with Miles,
 speedily perceived, at least, that it would give me a
1easure. No hour of my stay in fact was so assailed with
pprehensions as that of my coming down to learn that
1e carriage containing Mrs. Grose and my younger pupil
.ad already rolled out of the gates. Now I *was,* I said to
1yself, face to face with the elements, and for much of the
est of the day, while I fought my weakness, I could con-
ider that I had been supremely rash. It was a tighter
·lace still than I had yet turned round in; all the more
hat, for the first time, I could see in the aspect of others
 confused reflection of the crisis. What had happened
.aturally caused them all to stare; there was too little
·f the explained, throw out whatever we might, in the
uddenness of my colleague's act. The maids and the
1en looked blank; the effect of which on my nerves was
n aggravation until I saw the necessity of making it a
·ositive aid. It was precisely, in short, by just clutching
he helm that I avoided total wreck; and I dare say that, to
·ear up at all, I became, that morning, very grand and
ery dry. I welcomed the consciousness that I was charged
vith much to do, and I caused it to be known as well
hat, left thus to myself, I was quite remarkably firm. I
·andered with that manner, for the next hour or two, all
·ver the place and looked, I have no doubt, as if I were
eady for any onset. So, for the benefit of whom it might
oncern, I paraded with a sick heart.

The person it appeared least to concern proved to be,
ill dinner, little Miles himself. My perambulations had

given me meanwhile, no glimpse of him, but they ha
tended to make more public the change taking place in ou
relation as a consequence of his having at the piano, th
day before, kept me, in Flora's interest, so beguiled an
befooled. The stamp of publicity had of course been full
given by her confinement and departure, and the chang
itself was now ushered in by our non-observance of th
regular custom of the schoolroom. He had already di
appeared when, on my way down, I pushed open his doo
and I learned below that he had breakfasted—in the pre
ence of a couple of the maids—with Mrs. Grose and h
sister. He had then gone out, as he said, for a stroll; tha
which nothing, I reflected, could better have expressed h
frank view of the abrupt transformation of my offic
What he would now permit this office to consist of w
yet to be settled: there was a queer relief, at all events—
mean for myself in especial—in the renouncement of on
pretension. If so much had sprung to the surface, I scarc
put it too strongly in saying that what had perhaps sprun
highest was the absurdity of our prolonging the fictio
that I had anything more to teach him. It sufficient
stuck out that, by tacit little tricks in which even mor
than myself he carried out the care for my dignity, I ha
had to appeal to him to let me off straining to meet hir
on the ground of his true capacity. He had at any rate h
freedom now; I was never to touch it again; as I ha
amply shown, moreover, when, on his joining me in th
schoolroom the previous night, I had uttered, on the sul
ject of the interval just concluded, neither challenge no
hint. I had too much, from this moment, my other idea
Yet when he at last arrived the difficulty of applying ther
the accumulations of my problem, were brought straig
home to me by the beautiful little presence on whic
what had occurred had as yet, for the eye, dropped neithe
stain nor shadow.

To mark, for the house, the high state I cultivated
decreed that my meals with the boy should be served,
we called it, downstairs; so that I had been awaiting hir

in the ponderous pomp of the room outside of the window of which I had had from Mrs. Grose, that first scared Sunday, my flash of something it would scarce have done to call light. Here at present I felt afresh—for I had felt it again and again—how my equilibrium depended on the success of my rigid will, the will to shut my eyes as tight as possible to the truth that what I had to deal with was, revoltingly, against nature. I could only get on at all by taking "nature" into my confidence and my account, by treating my monstrous ordeal as a push in a direction unusual, of course, and unpleasant, but demanding, after all, for a fair front, only another turn of the screw of ordinary human virtue. No attempt, none the less, could well require more tact than just this attempt to supply, one's self, *all* the nature. How could I put even a little of that article into a suppression of reference to what had occurred? How, on the other hand, could I make a reference without a new plunge into the hideous obscure? Well, a sort of answer, after a time, had come to me, and it was so far confirmed as that I was met, incontestably, by the quickened vision of what was rare in my little companion. It was indeed as if he had found even now—as he had so often found at lessons—still some other delicate way to ease me off. Wasn't there light in the fact which, as we shared our solitude, broke out with a specious glitter it had never yet quite worn?—the fact that (opportunity aiding, precious opportunity which had now come) it would be preposterous, with a child so endowed, to forgo the help one might wrest from absolute intelligence? What had his intelligence been given him for but to save him? Mightn't one, to reach his mind, risk the stretch of an angular arm over his character? It was as if, when we were face to face in the dining-room, he had literally shown me the way. The roast mutton was on the table, and I had dispensed with attendance. Miles, before he sat down, stood a moment with his hands in his pockets and looked at the joint, on which he seemed on the point of passing some humorous judgment. But what he presently

produced was: "I say, my dear, is she really very awfull[
ill?"

"Little Flora? Not so bad but that she'll presently b
better. London will set her up. Bly had ceased to agre
with her. Come here and take your mutton."

He alertly obeyed me, carried the plate carefully to hi
seat, and, when he was established, went on. "Did Bl
disagree with her so terribly suddenly?"

"Not so suddenly as you might think. One had seen i
coming on."

"Then why didn't you get her off before?"

"Before what?"

"Before she became too ill to travel."

I found myself prompt. "She's *not* too ill to travel: sh
only might have become so if she had stayed. This wa
just the moment to seize. The journey will dissipate th
influence"—oh, I was grand!—"and carry it off."

"I see, I see"—Miles, for that matter, was grand too
He settled to his repast with the charming little "tabl
manner" that, from the day of his arrival, had relieve
me of all grossness of admonition. Whatever he had bee
driven from school for, it was not for ugly feeding. H
was irreproachable, as always, today; but he was unmi
takeably more conscious. He was discernibly trying t
take for granted more things than he found, without assis
ance, quite easy; and he dropped into peaceful silenc
while he felt his situation. Our meal was of the briefes
—mine a vain pretence, and I had the things immediatel
removed. While this was done Miles stood again with hi
hands in his little pockets and his back to me—stood an
looked out of the wide window through which, that othe
day, I had seen what pulled me up. We continued siler
while the maid was with us—as silent, it whimsically o
curred to me, as some young couple who, on their weddin
journey, at the inn, feel shy in the presence of the waite
He turned round only when the waiter had left us. "We
—so we're alone!"

OH, MORE OR LESS." I fancy my smile was pale. "Not absolutely. We shouldn't like that!" I went on.

"No—I suppose we shouldn't. Of course we have the others."

"We have the others—we have indeed the others," I concurred.

"Yet even though we have them," he returned, still with his hands in his pockets and planted there in front of me, "they don't much count, do they?"

I made the best of it, but I felt wan. "It depends on what you call 'much'!"

"Yes"—with all accommodation—"everything depends!" On this, however, he faced to the window again and presently reached it with his vague, restless, cogitating step. He remained there awhile, with his forehead against the glass, in contemplation of the stupid shrubs I knew and the dull things of November. I had always my hypocrisy of "work," behind which, now, I gained the sofa. Steadying myself with it there as I had repeatedly done at those moments of torment that I have described as the moments of my knowing the children to be given to something from which I was barred, I sufficiently obeyed my habit of being prepared for the worst. But an extraordinary impression dropped on me as I extracted a meaning from the boy's embarrassed back—none other than the impression that I was not barred now. This inference grew in a few minutes to sharp intensity and seemed bound up with the direct perception that it was positively he who was. The frames and squares of the great window were a kind of image, for him, of a kind of failure. I felt that I saw him, at any rate, shut in or shut out. He was admirable, but not comfortable: I took it in with a throb of hope. Wasn't he looking, through the haunted pane, for

117

something he couldn't see?—and wasn't it the first tim
in the whole business that he had known such a lapse
The first, the very first: I found it a splendid portent. I
made him anxious, though he watched himself; he ha
been anxious all day and, even while in his usual swee
little manner he sat at table, had needed all his sma
strange genius to give it a gloss. When he at last turne
round to meet me, it was almost as if this genius ha
succumbed. "Well, I think I'm glad Bly agrees with *me!*

"You would certainly seem to have seen, these twent
four hours, a good deal more of it than for some time be
fore. I hope," I went on bravely, "that you've been enjo
ing yourself."

"Oh, yes, I've been ever so far; all round about—mile
and miles away. I've never been so free."

He had really a manner of his own, and I could only tr
to keep up with him. "Well, do you like it?"

He stood there smiling; then at last he put into tw
words—"Do *you?*"—more discrimination than I had eve
heard two words contain. Before I had time to deal wit
that, however, he continued as if with the sense that th
was an impertinence to be softened. "Nothing could b
more charming than the way you take it, for of course
we're alone together now it's you that are alone mos
But I hope," he threw in, "you don't particularly mind!

"Having to do with you?" I asked. "My dear child, ho
can I help minding? Though I've renounced all claim t
your company,—you're so beyond me,—I at least great
enjoy it. What else should I stay on for?"

He looked at me more directly, and the expression c
his face, graver now, struck me as the most beautiful
had ever found in it. "You stay on just for *that?*"

"Certainly. I stay on as your friend and from the tre
mendous interest I take in you till something can be don
for you that may be more worth your while. That needn
surprise you." My voice trembled so that I felt it impossib
to suppress the shake. "Don't you remember how I tol
you, when I came and sat on your bed the night c

the storm, that there was nothing in the world I wouldn't do for you?"

"Yes, yes!" He, on his side, more and more visibly nervous, had a tone to master; but he was so much more successful than I that, laughing out through his gravity, he could pretend we were pleasantly jesting. "Only that, I think, was to get me to do something for *you!*"

"It was partly to get you to do something," I conceded. "But, you know, you didn't do it."

"Oh, yes," he said with the brightest superficial eagerness, "you wanted me to tell you something."

"That's it. Out, straight out. What you have on your mind, you know."

"Ah, then, is *that* what you've stayed over for?"

He spoke with a gaiety through which I could still catch the finest little quiver of resentful passion; but I can't begin to express the effect upon me of an implication of surrender even so faint. It was as if what I had yearned for had come at last only to astonish me. "Well, yes—I may as well make a clean breast of it. It was precisely for that."

He waited so long that I supposed it for the purpose of repudiating the assumption on which my action had been founded; but what he finally said was: "Do you mean now—here?"

"There couldn't be a better place or time." He looked round him uneasily, and I had the rare—oh, the queer!—impression of the very first symptom I had seen in him of the approach of immediate fear. It was as if he were suddenly afraid of me—which struck me indeed as perhaps the best thing to make him. Yet in the very pang of the effort I felt it vain to try sternness, and I heard myself the next instant so gentle as to be almost grotesque. "You want so to go out again?"

"Awfully!" He smiled at me heroically, and the touching little bravery of it was enhanced by his actually flushing with pain. He had picked up his hat, which he had brought in, and stood twirling it in a way that gave me, even as I was just nearly reaching port, a perverse horror of what I was doing. To do it in *any* way was an act of violence, for what did it consist of but the obtrusion of the idea of grossness and guilt on a small helpless creature who had been for me a revelation of the possibilities of beautiful intercourse? Wasn't it base to create for a being so exquisite a mere alien awkwardness? I suppose I now read into our situation a clearness it couldn't have had at the time, for I seem to see our poor eyes already lighted with some spark of a prevision of the anguish that was to come. So we circled about, with terrors and scruples, like fighters not daring to close. But it was for each other we feared! That kept us a little longer suspended and unbruised. "I'll tell you everything," Miles said—"I mean I'll tell you anything you like. You'll stay on with me, and we shall both be all right and I *will* tell you—I *will*. But not now."

"Why not now?"

My insistence turned him from me and kept him once more at his window in a silence during which, between us, you might have heard a pin drop. Then he was before me again with the air of a person for whom, outside, someone who had frankly to be reckoned with was waiting. "I have to see Luke."

I had not yet reduced him to quite so vulgar a lie, and I felt proportionately ashamed. But, horrible as it was, his lies made up my truth. I achieved thoughtfully a few loops of my knitting. "Well, then, go to Luke, and I'll wait for what you promise. Only, in return for that, satisfy, before you leave me, one very much smaller request."

He looked as if he felt he had succeeded enough to be able still a little to bargain. "Very much smaller—?"

"Yes, a mere fraction of the whole. Tell me"—oh, my work preoccupied me, and I was off-hand!—"if, yesterday afternoon, from the table in the hall, you took, you know, my letter."

24

Y SENSE OF HOW HE RECEIVED THIS suffered for a minute
om something that I can describe only as a fierce split
my attention—a stroke that at first, as I sprang straight
o, reduced me to the mere blind movement of getting
old of him, drawing him close, and, while I just fell for
pport against the nearest piece of furniture, instinc-
vely keeping him with his back to the window. The
ppearance was full upon us that I had already had to
eal with here: Peter Quint had come into view like a
ntinel before a prison. The next thing I saw was that,
om outside, he had reached the window, and then I knew
at, close to the glass and glaring in through it, he offered
nce more to the room his white face of damnation. It
presents but grossly what took place within me at the
ght to say that on the second my decision was made; yet
believe that no woman so overwhelmed ever in so short
time recovered her grasp of the *act*. It came to me in
e very horror of the immediate presence that the act
ould be, seeing and facing what I saw and faced, to keep
e boy himself unaware. The inspiration—I can call it
no other name—was that I felt how voluntarily, how
anscendently, I *might*. It was like fighting with a demon
r a human soul, and when I had fairly so appraised it I
w how the human soul—held out, in the tremor of my
nds, at arm's length—had a perfect dew of sweat on a
vely childish forehead. The face that was close to mine
as as white as the face against the glass, and out of it
esently came a sound, not low nor weak, but as if from
uch further away, that I drank like a waft of fragrance.
"Yes—I took it."

At this, with a moan of joy, I enfolded, I drew him
ose; and while I held him to my breast, where I could
el in the sudden fever of his little body the tremendous

121

pulse of his little heart, I kept my eyes on the thing at th
window and saw it move and shift its posture. I hav
likened it to a sentinel, but its slow wheel, for a momen
was rather the prowl of a baffled beast. My present quic
ened courage, however, was such that, not too much to l
it through, I had to shade, as it were, my flame. Mea
while the glare of the face was again at the window, th
scoundrel fixed as if to watch and wait. It was the ver
confidence that I might now defy him, as well as the pos
tive certitude, by this time, of the child's unconsciousnes
that made me go on. "What did you take it for?"

"To see what you said about me."

"You opened the letter?"

"I opened it."

My eyes were now, as I held him off a little again, o
Miles's own face, in which the collapse of mockery showe
me how complete was the ravage of uneasiness. What wa
prodigious was that at last, by my success, his sense wa
sealed and his communication stopped: he knew that h
was in presence, but knew not of what, and knew sti
less that I also was and that I did know. And what did th
strain of trouble matter when my eyes went back to th
window only to see that the air was clear again and—b
my personal triumph—the influence quenched? There wa
nothing there. I felt that the cause was mine and that
should surely get *all*. "And you found nothing!"—I let m
elation out.

He gave the most mournful, thoughtful little hea
shake. "Nothing."

"Nothing, nothing!" I almost shouted in my joy.

"Nothing, nothing," he sadly repeated.

I kissed his forehead; it was drenched. "So what hav
you done with it?"

"I've burnt it."

"Burnt it?" It was now or never. "Is that what you di
at school?"

Oh, what this brought up! "At school?"

"Did you take letters?—or other things?"

"Other things?" He appeared now to be thinking of something far off and that reached him only through the pressure of his anxiety. Yet it did reach him. "Did I *steal?*"

I felt myself redden to the roots of my hair as well as wonder if it were more strange to put to a gentleman such a question or to see him take it with allowances that gave the very distance of his fall in the world. "Was it for that you mightn't go back?"

The only thing he felt was rather a dreary little surprise. "Did you know I mightn't go back?"

"I know everything."

He gave me at this the longest and strangest look. "Everything?"

"Everything. Therefore *did* you—?" But I couldn't say it again.

Miles could, very simply. "No. I didn't steal."

My face must have shown him I believed him utterly; yet my hands—but it was for pure tenderness—shook him as if to ask him why, if it was all for nothing, he had condemned me to months of torment. "What then did you do?"

He looked in vague pain all round the top of the room and drew his breath, two or three times over, as if with difficulty. He might have been standing at the bottom of the sea and raising his eyes to some faint green twilight. "Well—I said things."

"Only that?"

"They thought it was enough!"

"To turn you out for?"

Never, truly, had a person "turned out" shown so little to explain it as this little person! He appeared to weigh my question, but in a manner quite detached and almost helpless. "Well, I suppose I oughtn't."

"But to whom did you say them?"

He evidently tried to remember, but it dropped—he had lost it. "I don't know!"

He almost smiled at me in the desolation of his surrender, which was indeed practically, by this time, so complete that I ought to have left it there. But I was infatuated—I was blind with victory, though even then the very effect that was to have brought him so much nearer was already that of added separation. "Was it to everyone?" I asked.

"No; it was only to—" But he gave a sick little head-shake. "I don't remember their names."

"Were they then so many?"

"No—only a few. Those I liked."

Those he liked? I seemed to float not into clearness, but into a darker obscure, and within a minute there had come to me out of my very pity the appalling alarm of his being perhaps innocent. It was for the instant confounding and bottomless, for if he *were* innocent, what then on earth was *I*? Paralysed, while it lasted, by the mere brush of the question, I let him go a little, so that, with a deep-drawn sigh, he turned away from me again; which, as he faced toward the clear window, I suffered, feeling that I had nothing now there to keep him from. "And did they repeat what you said?" I went on after a moment.

He was soon at some distance from me, still breathing hard and again with the air, though now without anger for it, of being confined against his will. Once more, as he had done before, he looked up at the dim day as if, of what had hitherto sustained him, nothing was left but an unspeakable anxiety. "Oh, yes," he nevertheless replied—"they must have repeated them. To those *they* liked," he added.

There was, somehow, less of it than I had expected; but I turned it over. "And these things came round—?"

"To the masters? Oh, yes!" he answered very simply. "But I didn't know they'd tell."

"The masters? They didn't—they've never told. That's why I ask you."

He turned to me again his little beautiful fevered face. "Yes, it was too bad."

"Too bad?"

"What I suppose I sometimes said. To write home."

I can't name the exquisite pathos of the contradiction given to such a speech by such a speaker; I only know that the next instant I heard myself throw off with homely force: "Stuff and nonsense!" But the next after that I must have sounded stern enough. "What were these things?"

My sternness was all for his judge, his executioner; yet it made him avert himself again, and that movement made *me*, with a single bound and an irrepressible cry, spring straight upon him. For there again, against the glass, as if to blight his confession and stay his answer, was the hideous author of our woe—the white face of damnation. I felt a sick swim at the drop of my victory and all the return of my battle, so that the wildness of my verible leap only served as a great betrayal. I saw him, from the midst of my act, meet it with a divination, and on the perception that even now he only guessed, and that the window was still to his own eyes free, I let the impulse came up to convert the climax of his dismay into the very proof of his liberation. "No more, no more, no more!" I shrieked, as I tried to press him against me, to my visitant.

"Is she *here*?" Miles panted as he caught with his sealed eyes the direction of my words. Then as his strange "she" staggered me and, with a gasp, I echoed it, "Miss Jessel, Miss Jessel!" he with a sudden fury gave me back.

I seized, stupefied, his supposition—some sequel to what we had done to Flora, but this made me only want to show him that it was better still than that. "It's not Miss Jessel! But it's at the window—straight before us. It's *there*—the coward horror, there for the last time!"

At this, after a second in which his head made the movement of a baffled dog's on a scent and then gave a frantic little shake for air and light, he was at me in a white rage, bewildered, glaring vainly over the place and missing wholly, though it now, to my sense, filled the room like the taste of poison, the wide, overwhelming presence. It's *he*?"

I was so determined to have all my proof that I flashed

into ice to challenge him. "Whom do you mean by 'he'".

"Peter Quint—you devil!" His face gave again, roun the room, its convulsed supplication. *"Where?"*

They are in my ears still, his supreme surrender of th name and his tribute to my devotion. "What does h matter now, my own?—what will he *ever* matter? *I* ha you," I launched at the beast, "but he has lost you fe ever!" Then, for the demonstration of my work, "Ther *there!*" I said to Miles.

But he had already jerked straight round, stared, glare again, and seen but the quiet day. With the stroke of th loss I was so proud of he uttered the cry of a creatur hurled over an abyss, and the grasp with which I reco ered him might have been that of catching him in his fa I caught him, yes, I held him—it may be imagined wit what a passion; but at the end of a minute I began to fe what it truly was that I held. We were alone with the qui day, and his little heart, dispossessed, had stopped.

● ● ●

DAISY MILLER

1

Les Trois Couronnes

AT THE LITTLE TOWN OF VEVAY, in Switzerland, there is a particularly comfortable hotel. There are, indeed, many hotels; for the entertainment of tourists is the business of the place, which, as many travellers will remember, is seated upon the edge of a remarkably blue lake—a lake that it behooves every tourist to visit. The shore of the lake presents an unbroken array of establishments of this order, of every category, from the "grand hotel" of the newest fashion, with a chalk-white front, a hundred balconies, and a dozen flags flying from its roof, to the little Swiss *pension* of an elder day, with its name inscribed in German-looking lettering upon a pink or yellow wall, and an awkward summer-house in the angle of the garden. One of the hotels at Vevay, however, is famous, even classical, being distinguished from any of its upstart neighbors by an air both of luxury and of maturity. In this region, in the month of June, American travellers are extremely numerous; it may be said, indeed, that Vevay assumes at this period some of the characteristics of an American watering-place. There are sights and sounds which evoke a vision, an echo, of Newport and Saratoga. There is a flitting hither and thither of "stylish" young girls, a rustling of muslin flounces, a rattle of dance-music in the morning hours, a sound of high-pitched voices at all times. You receive an impression of these things at the excellent inn of the Trois Couronnes, and are transported in fancy to the Ocean House or to Congress Hall. But at the Trois Couronnes, it must

be added, there are other features that are much at vari
ance with these suggestions: neat German waiters, wh
look like secretaries of legation, Russian princesses sittin
in the garden; little Polish boys walking about, held b
the hand, with their governors; a view of the sunny cres
of the Dent du Midi and the picturesque towers of th
Castle of Chillon.

I hardly know whether it was the analogies or th
differences that were uppermost in the mind of a youn
American, who, two or three years ago, sat in the garden
of the Trois Couronnes, looking about him, rather idly
at some of the graceful objects I have mentioned. It wa
a beautiful summer morning, and in whatever fashion th
young American looked at things they must have seeme
to him charming. He had come from Geneva the da
before by the little steamer to see his aunt, who wa
staying at the hotel—Geneva having been for a long tim
his place of residence. But his aunt had a headache—hi
aunt had almost always a headache—and now she wa
shut up in her room, smelling camphor, so that he wa
at liberty to wander about. He was some seven-and-twent
years of age. When his friends spoke of him, they usuall
said that he "was at Geneva studying"; when his enemie
spoke of him, they said—but, after all, he had no enemies
he was an extremely amiable fellow, and universally liked
What I should say is, simply, that when certain person
spoke of him they affirmed that the reason of his spendin
so much time at Geneva was that he was extremely de
voted to a lady who lived there—a foreign lady—a perso
older than himself. Very few Americans—indeed, I thin
none—had ever seen this lady, about whom there wer
some singular stories. But Winterbourne had an ol
attachment for the little metropolis of Calvinism; he ha
been put to school there as a boy, and he had afterward
gone to college there—circumstances which had led t
his forming a great many youthful friendships. Many c
these he had kept, and they were a source of great sati
faction to him.

After knocking at his aunt's door, and learning that she was indisposed, he had taken a walk about the town, and then he had come in to his breakfast. He had now finished his breakfast; but he was drinking a small cup of coffee, which had been served to him on a little table in the garden by one of the waiters who looked like an attaché. At last he finished his coffee and lit a cigarette. Presently a small boy came walking along the path—an urchin of nine or ten. The child, who was diminutive for his years, had an aged expression of countenance: a pale complexion, and sharp little features. He was dressed in knickerbockers, with red stockings, which displayed his poor little spindle-shanks; he also wore a brilliant red cravat. He carried in his hand a long alpenstock, the sharp point of which he thrust into everything that he approached—the flower-beds, the garden-benches, the trains of the ladies' dresses. In front of Winterbourne he paused, looking at him with a pair of bright, penetrating little eyes.

"Will you give me a lump of sugar?" he asked, in a sharp, hard little voice—a voice immature, and yet, somehow, not young.

Winterbourne glanced at the small table near him, on which his coffee-service rested, and saw that several morsels of sugar remained. "Yes, you may take one," he answered; "but I don't think sugar is good for little boys."

This little boy stepped forward and carefully selected three of the coveted fragments, two of which he buried in the pocket of his knickerbockers, depositing the other as promptly in another place. He poked his alpenstock, lance-fashion, into Winterbourne's bench, and tried to crack the lump of sugar with his teeth.

"Oh, blazes; it's har-r-d!" he exclaimed, pronouncing the adjective in a peculiar manner.

Winterbourne had immediately perceived that he might have the honor of claiming him as a fellow-countryman. "Take care you don't hurt your teeth," he said, paternally.

"I haven't got any teeth to hurt. They have all come out. I have only got seven teeth. My mother counted them last night, and one came out right afterwards. She said she'd slap me if any more came out. I can't help it. It's this old Europe. It's the climate that makes them come out. In America they didn't come out. It's these hotels."

Winterbourne was much amused. "If you eat three lumps of sugar, your mother will certainly slap you," he said.

"She's got to give me some candy, then," rejoined his young interlocutor. "I can't get any candy here—any American candy. American candy's the best candy."

"And are American little boys the best little boys?" asked Winterbourne.

"I don't know. I'm an American boy," said the child.

"I see you are one of the best!" laughed Winterbourne.

"Are you an American man?" pursued this vivacious infant. And then, on Winterbourne's affirmative reply—"American men are the best!" he declared.

His companion thanked him for the compliment; and the child, who had now got astride his alpenstock, stood looking about him, while he attacked a second lump of sugar. Winterbourne wondered if he himself had been like this in his infancy, for he had been brought to Europe at about this age.

"Here comes my sister!" cried the child, in a moment. "She's an American girl."

Winterbourne looked along the path and saw a beautiful young lady advancing. "American girls are the best girls!" he said, cheerfully, to his young companion.

"My sister ain't the best!" the child declared. "She's always blowing at me."

"I imagine that is your fault, not hers," said Winterbourne. The young lady meanwhile had drawn near. She was dressed in white muslin, with a hundred frills and flounces, and knots of pale-colored ribbon. She was bareheaded; but she balanced in her hand a large para

130

sol, with a deep border of embroidery; and she was strikingly, admirably pretty. "How pretty they are!" thought Winterbourne, straightening himself in his seat, as if he were prepared to rise.

The young lady paused in front of his bench, near the parapet of the garden, which overlooked the lake. The little boy had now converted his alpenstock into a vaulting-pole, by the aid of which he was springing about in the gravel, and kicking it up a little.

"Randolph," said the young lady, "what *are* you doing?"

"I'm going up the Alps," replied Randolph. "This is the way!" And he gave another little jump, scattering the pebbles about Winterbourne's ears.

"That's the way they come down," said Winterbourne.

"He's an American man!" cried Randolph, in his hard little voice.

The young lady gave no heed to this announcement, but looked straight at her brother. "Well, I guess you had better be quiet," she simply observed.

It seemed to Winterbourne that he had been in a manner presented. He got up and stepped slowly towards the young girl, throwing away his cigarette. "This little boy and I have made acquaintance," he said, with great civility. In Geneva, as he had been perfectly aware, a young man was not at liberty to speak to a young unmarried lady except under certain rarely occurring conditions; but here at Vevay, what conditions could be better than these?—a pretty American girl coming and standing in front of you in a garden. This pretty American girl, however, on hearing Winterbourne's observation, simply glanced at him; she then turned her head and looked over the parapet, at the lake and the opposite mountains. He wondered whether he had gone too far; but he decided that he must advance farther, rather than retreat. While he was thinking of something else to say, the young lady turned to the little boy again.

"I should like to know where you got that pole?" she said.

"I bought it," responded Randolph.

"You don't mean to say you're going to take it to Italy?"

"Yes, I am going to take it to Italy," the child declared.

The young girl glanced over the front of her dress, and smoothed out a knot or two of ribbon. Then she rested her eyes upon the prospect again. "Well, guess you had better leave it somewhere," she said, after a moment.

"Are you going to Italy?" Winterbourne inquired, in a tone of great respect.

The young lady glanced at him again. "Yes, sir," she replied. And she said nothing more.

"Are you—a—going over the Simplon?" Winterbourne pursued, a little embarrassed.

"I don't know," she said. "I suppose it's some mountain. Randolph, what mountain are we going over?"

"Going where?" the child demanded.

"To Italy," Winterbourne explained.

"I don't know," said Randolph. "I don't want to go to Italy. I want to go to America."

"Oh, Italy is a beautiful place!" rejoined the young man.

"Can you get candy there?" Randolph loudly inquired.

"I hope not," said his sister. "I guess you have had enough candy, and mother thinks so, too."

"I haven't had any for ever so long—for a hundred weeks!" cried the boy, still jumping about.

The young lady inspected her flounces and smoothed her ribbons again, and Winterbourne presently risked an observation upon the beauty of the view. He was ceasing to be embarrassed, for he had begun to perceive that she was not in the least embarrassed herself. There had not been the slightest alteration in her charming complexion; she was evidently neither offended nor fluttered. If she looked another way when he spoke to her, and seemed not particularly to hear him, this was simply her habit, her manner. Yet, as he talked a little more, and pointed out some of the objects of interest in the view, with which she appeared quite unacquainted, she gradually gave him more of the benefit of her glance; and then he saw that this glance was perfectly direct and unshrinking. It was not, however, what would have been called an immodest glance, for the young girl's eyes were singularly honest and fresh. They were wonderfully pretty eyes; and, indeed, Winterbourne had not seen for a long time anything prettier than his fair countrywoman's various features—her complexion, her nose, her ears, her teeth. He had a great relish for feminine beauty; he was addicted to observing and analyzing it; and as regards this young lady's face he made several observations. It was not at all insipid, but it was not exactly expressive; and though it was eminently delicate, Winterbourne mentally accused it—very forgivingly—of a want of finish. He thought it very possible that Master Randolph's sister was a coquette; he was sure she had a spirit of her own; but in her bright, sweet, superficial little visage there was no mockery, no irony. Before long it became obvious that she was much disposed towards conversation. She told him that they were going to Rome for the winter—she and her mother and Randolph. She asked him if he was a "real American"; she shouldn't have taken him for one; he seemed more like a German—this was said after a little hesitation—especially when he spoke. Winterbourne, laughing, answered that he had met Germans who spoke like Americans; but that he had not, so far as he remembered, met an American who spoke like a German. Then he asked her if she should not be more comfortable in sitting upon the bench which he had just quitted. She answered that she liked standing up and walking about; but she presently sat down. She told him she was from New York State—"if you know where that is." Winterbourne learned more about her by catching hold of her small, slippery brother, and making him stand a few minutes by his side.

"Tell me your name, my boy," he said.

"Randolph C. Miller," said the boy, sharply. "And I'll tell you her name;" and he levelled his alpenstock at his sister.

"You had better wait till you are asked!" said this young lady, calmly.

"I should like very much to know your name," said Winterbourne.

"Her name is Daisy Miller!" cried the child. "But that isn't her real name; that isn't her name on her cards."

"It's a pity you haven't got one of my cards!" said Miss Miller.

"Her real name is Annie P. Miller," the boy went on.

"Ask him *his* name," said his sister, indicating Winterbourne.

But on this point Randolph seemed perfectly indifferent; he continued to supply information with regard to his own family. "My father's name is Ezra B. Miller," he announced. "My father ain't in Europe; my father's in a better place than Europe."

Winterbourne imagined for a moment that this was the manner in which the child had been taught to intimate that Mr. Miller had been removed to the sphere of celestial rewards. But Randolph immediately added, "My father's in Schenectady. He's got a big business. My father's rich, you bet!"

"Well!" ejaculated Miss Miller, lowering her parasol and looking at the embroidered border. Winterbourne presently released the child, who departed, dragging his alpenstock along the path. "He doesn't like Europe," said the young girl. "He wants to go back."

"To Schenectady, you mean?"

"Yes; he wants to go right home. He hasn't got any boys here. There is one boy here, but he always goes round with a teacher; they won't let him play."

"And your brother hasn't any teacher?" Winterbourne inquired.

"Mother thought of getting him one to travel round with us. There was a lady told her of a very good teacher;

n American lady—perhaps you know her—Mrs. Sanders.
think she came from Boston. She told her of this teacher,
nd we thought of getting him to travel round with us.
But Randolph said he didn't want a teacher travelling
ound with us. He said he wouldn't have lessons when
e was in the cars. And we *are* in the cars about half the
ime. There was an English lady we met in the cars—I
hink her name was Miss Featherstone; perhaps you know
er. She wanted to know why I didn't give Randolph
essons—give him 'instructions,' she called it. I guess he
ould give me more instruction than I could give him.
He's very smart."

"Yes," said Winterbourne; "he seems very smart."

"Mother's going to get a teacher for him as soon as
ve get to Italy. Can you get good teachers in Italy?"

"Very good, I should think," said Winterbourne.

"Or else she's going to find some school. He ought to
earn some more. He's only nine. He's going to college."
And in this way Miss Miller continued to converse upon
he affairs of her family, and upon other topics. She sat
here with her extremely pretty hands, ornamented with
ery brilliant rings, folded in her lap, and with her pretty
yes now resting upon those of Winterbourne, now wandering over the garden, the people who passed by, and
he beautiful view. She talked to Winterbourne as if she
ad known him a long time. He found it very pleasant.
t was many years since he had heard a young girl talk so
much. It might have been said of this unknown young
ady, who had come and sat down beside him upon a
bench, that she chattered. She was very quiet; she sat in a
harming, tranquil attitude, but her lips and her eyes
vere constantly moving. She had a soft, slender, agreeable
oice, and her tone was decidedly sociable. She gave Winterbourne a history of her movements and intentions, and
hose of her mother and brother, in Europe, and enumer-
ted, in particular, the various hotels at which they had
topped. "That English lady in the cars," she said—"Miss
featherstone—asked me if we didn't all live in hotels in

America. I told her I had never been in so many hotels in my life as since I came to Europe. I have never seen so many—it's nothing but hotels." But Miss Miller did not make this remark with a querulous accent; she appeared to be in the best humor with everything. She declared that the hotels were very good, when once you got used to their ways, and that Europe was perfectly sweet. She was not disappointed—not a bit. Perhaps it was because she had heard so much about it before. She had ever so many intimate friends that had been there ever so many times. And then she had ever so many dresses and things from Paris. Whenever she put on a Paris dress she felt as if she were in Europe.

"It was a kind of a wishing-cap," said Winterbourne.

"Yes," said Miss Miller, without examining this analogy; "it always made me wish I was here. But I needn't have done that for dresses. I am sure they send all the pretty ones to America; you see the most frightful things here. The only thing I don't like," she proceeded, "is the society. There isn't any society; or, if there is, I don't know where it keeps itself. Do you? I suppose there is some society somewhere, but I haven't seen anything of it. I'm very fond of society, and I have always had a great deal of it. I don't mean only in Schenectady, but in New York. I used to go to New York every winter. In New York I had lots of society. Last winter I had seventeen dinners given me; and three of them were by gentlemen," added Daisy Miller. "I have more friends in New York than in Schenectady—more gentlemen friends; and more young lady friends, too," she resumed in a moment. She paused again for an instant; she was looking at Winterbourne with all her prettiness in her lively eyes, and in her light, slightly monotonous smile. "I have always had," she said, "a great deal of gentlemen's society."

Poor Winterbourne was amused, perplexed, and decidedly charmed. He had never yet heard a young girl express herself in just this fashion—never, at least, save in cases where to say such things seemed a kind of de-

onstrative evidence of a certain laxity of deportment.
nd yet was he to accuse Miss Daisy Miller of actual or
otential *inconduite,* as they said at Geneva? He felt that
e had lived at Geneva so long that he had lost a good
eal; he had become dishabituated to the American tone.
ever, indeed, since he had grown old enough to appre-
ate things had he encountered a young American girl
so pronounced a type as this. Certainly she was very
harming, but how deucedly sociable! Was she simply
pretty girl from New York State? Were they all like that,
he pretty girls who had a good deal of gentlemen's so-
ety? Or was she also a designing, an audacious, an un-
rupulous young person? Winterbourne had lost his
stinct in this matter, and his reason could not help
im. Miss Daisy Miller looked extremely innocent. Some
eople had told him that, after all, American girls were
xceedingly innocent; and others had told him that,
ter all, they were not. He was inclined to think Miss
aisy Miller was a flirt—a pretty American flirt. He had
ever, as yet, had any relations with young ladies of this
ategory. He had known, here in Europe, two or three
omen—persons older than Miss Daisy Miller, and pro-
ded, for respectability's sake, with husbands—who were
eat coquettes—dangerous, terrible women, with whom
ne's relations were liable to take a serious turn. But this
oung girl was not a coquette in that sense; she was very
nsophisticated; she was only a pretty American flirt.
Vinterbourne was almost grateful for having found the
rmula that applied to Miss Daisy Miller. He leaned
ack in his seat; he remarked to himself that she had the
ost charming nose he had ever seen; he wondered what
ere the regular conditions and limitations of one's inter-
ourse with a pretty American flirt. It presently became
oparent that he was on the way to learn.

"Have you been to that old castle?" asked the young
rl, pointing with her parasol to the far-gleaming walls
the Château de Chillon.

"Yes, formerly, more than once," said Winterbourne.

"You, too, I suppose, have seen it?"

"No; we haven't been there. I want to go there dread
fully. Of course I mean to go there. I wouldn't go awa
from here without having seen that old castle."

"It's a very pretty excursion," said Winterbourne, "an
very easy to make. You can drive or go by the littl
steamer."

"You can go in the cars," said Miss Miller.

"Yes; you can go in the cars," Winterbourne assented

"Our courier says they take you right up to the castle,
the young girl continued. "We were going last week; bu
my mother gave out. She suffers dreadfully from dyspepsi
She said she couldn't go. Randolph wouldn't go, eithe
he say he doesn't think much of old castles. But I gues
we'll go this week, if we can get Randolph."

"Your brother is not interested in ancient monuments?"
Winterbourne inquired, smiling.

"He says he don't care much about old castles. He
only nine. He wants to stay at the hotel. Mother's afrai
to leave him alone, and the courier won't stay with him
so we haven't been to many places. But it will be too ba
if we don't go up there." And Miss Miller pointed agai
at the Château de Chillon.

"I should think it might be arranged," said Winte
bourne. "Couldn't you get some one to stay for the afte
noon with Randolph?"

Miss Miller looked at him a moment, and then ver
placidly, "I wish *you* would stay with him!" she said.

Winterbourne hesitated a moment. "I should muc
rather go to Chillon with you."

"With me?" asked the young girl, with the sam
placidity.

She didn't rise, blushing, as a young girl at Genev
would have done; and yet Winterbourne, conscious th
he had been very bold, thought it possible that she w
offended. "With your mother," he answered, very respec
fully.

But it seemed that both his audacity and his respe

were lost upon Miss Daisy Miller. "I guess my mother won't go, after all," she said. "She don't like to ride round in the afternoon. But did you really mean what you said just now, that you would like to go up there?"

"Most earnestly," Winterbourne declared.

"Then we may arrange it. If mother will stay with Randolph, I guess Eugenio will."

"Eugenio?" the young man inquired.

"Eugenio's our courier. He doesn't like to stay with Randolph; he's the most fastidious man I ever saw. But he's a splendid courier. I guess he'll stay at home with Randolph if mother does, and then we can go to the castle."

Winterbourne reflected for an instant as lucidly as possible—"we" could only mean Miss Daisy Miller and himself. This programme seemed almost too agreeable for credence; he felt as if he ought to kiss the young lady's hand. Possibly he would have done so, and quite spoiled the project; but at this moment another person, presumably Eugenio, appeared. A tall, handsome man, with superb whiskers, wearing a velvet morning-coat and a brilliant watch-chain, approached Miss Miller, looking sharply at her companion. "Oh, Eugenio!" said Miss Miller, with the friendliest accent.

Eugenio had looked at Winterbourne from head to foot; he now bowed gravely to the young lady. "I have the honor to inform mademoiselle that luncheon is upon the table."

Miss Miller slowly rose. "See here, Eugenio!" she said; "I'm going to that old castle, anyway."

"To the Château de Chillon, mademoiselle?" the courier inquired. "Mademoiselle has made arrangements?" he added, in a tone which struck Winterbourne as very impertinent.

Eugenio's tone apparently threw, even to Miss Miller's own apprehension, a slightly ironical light upon the young girl's situation. She turned to Winterbourne, blushing a little—a very little. "You won't back out?" she said.

139

"I shall not be happy till we go!" he protested.

"And you are staying in this hotel?" she went on. "And you are really an American?"

The courier stood looking at Winterbourne offensively. The young man, at least, thought his manner of looking an offence to Miss Miller; it conveyed an imputation that she "picked up" acquaintances. "I shall have the honor of presenting to you a person who will tell you all about me," he said, smiling, and referring to his aunt.

"Oh, well, we'll go some day," said Miss Miller. And she gave him a smile and turned away. She put up her parasol and walked back to the inn beside Eugenio. Winterbourne stood looking after her; and as she moved away, drawing her muslin furbelows over the gravel, said to himself that she had the *tournure* of a princess.

He had, however, engaged to do more than proved feasible, in promising to present his aunt, Mrs. Costello, to Miss Daisy Miller. As soon as the former lady had got better of her headache he waited upon her in her apartment; and, after the proper inquiries in regard to her health, he asked her if she had observed in the hotel an American family—a mamma, a daughter, and a little boy.

"And a courier?" said Mrs. Costello. "Oh yes, I have observed them. Seen them—heard them—and kept out of their way." Mrs. Costello was a widow with a fortune, a person of much distinction, who frequently intimated that, if she were not so dreadfully liable to sick-headaches, she would probably have left a deeper impress upon her time. She had a long, pale face, a high nose, and a great deal of very striking white hair, which she wore in large puffs and *rouleaux* over the top of her head. She had two sons married in New York, and another who was now in Europe. This young man was amusing himself at Homburg; and, though he was on his travels, was rarely perceived to visit any particular city at the moment selected by his mother for her own appearance there. Her nephew, who had come up to Vevay expressly to see her, was there

140

ɔre more attentive than those who, as she said, were
ɛarer to her. He had imbibed at Geneva the idea that one
ꞁust always be attentive to one's aunt. Mrs. Costello had
ɔt seen him for many years, and she was greatly pleased
ʾith him, manifesting her approbation by initiating him
ꞁto many of the secrets of that social sway which, as she
ave him to understand, she exerted in the American capi-
ꞁl. She admitted that she was very exclusive; but, if he
ʾere acquainted with New York, he would see that one
ad to be. And her picture of the minutely hierarchical
ɔnstitution of the society of that city, which she presented
ɔ him in many different lights, was, to Winterbourne's
ꞁagination, almost oppressively striking.

He immediately perceived, from her tone, that Miss
ʾaisy Miller's place in the social scale was low. "I am
ꞁraid you don't approve of them," he said.

"They are very common," Mrs. Costello declared.
They are the sort of Americans that one does one's duty
y not—not accepting."

"Ah, you don't accept them?" said the young man.

"I can't, my dear Frederick. I would if I could, but I
ꞁn't."

"The young girl is very pretty," said Winterbourne, in
ꞁ moment.

"Of course she's pretty. But she is very common."

"I see what you mean, of course," said Winterbourne,
ꞁter another pause.

"She has that charming look that they all have," his
ꞁnt resumed. "I can't think where they pick it up; and
ꞁe dresses in perfection—no, you don't know how well
ꞁe dresses. I can't think where they get their taste."

"But, my dear aunt, she is not, after all, a Comanche
ꞁvage."

"She is a young lady," said Mrs. Costello, "who has
ꞁ intimacy with her mamma's courier."

"An intimacy with the courier?" the young man de-
ꞁanded.

"Oh, the mother is just as bad! They treat the courier

like a familiar friend—like a gentleman. I shouldn't won
der if he dines with them. Very likely they have neve
seen a man with such good manners, such fine clothe
so like a gentleman. He probably corresponds to the youn
lady's idea of a count. He sits with them in the garden i
the evening. I think he smokes."

Winterbourne listened with interest to these disclo
sures; they helped him to make up his mind about Mi
Daisy. Evidently she was rather wild.

"Well," he said, "I am not a courier, and yet she wa
very charming to me."

"You had better have said at first," said Mrs. Costell
with dignity, "that you had made her acquaintance."

"We simply met in the garden, and we talked a bit."

"*Tout bonnement!* And pray what did you say?"

"I said I should take the liberty of introducing her
my admirable aunt."

"I am much obliged to you."

"It was to guarantee my respectability," said Winte
bourne.

"And pray who is to guarantee hers?"

"Ah, you are cruel," said the young man. "She's a ve
nice young girl."

"You don't say that as if you believed it," Mrs. Co
tello observed.

"She is completely uncultivated," Winterbourne wen
on. "But she is wonderfully pretty, and, in short, she
very nice. To prove that I believe it, I am going to tal
her to the Château de Chillon."

"You two are going off there together? I should sa
it proved just the contrary. How long had you know
her, may I ask, when this interesting project was forme
You haven't been twenty-four hours in the house."

"I had known her half an hour!" said Winterbourn
smiling.

"Dear me!" cried Mrs. Costello. "What a dreadful girl

Her nephew was silent for some moments. "You rea
think, then," he began, earnestly, and with a desire f

trustworthy information—"you really think that—" But he paused again.

"Think what, sir?" said his aunt.

"That she is the sort of young lady who expects a man, sooner or later, to carry her off?"

"I haven't the least idea what such young ladies expect a man to do. But I really think that you had better not meddle with little American girls that are uncultivated, as you call them. You have lived too long out of the country. You will be sure to make some great mistake. You are too innocent."

"My dear aunt, I am not so innocent," said Winterbourne, smiling and curling his mustache.

"You are too guilty, then!"

Winterbourne continued to curl his mustache, mediatively. "You won't let the poor girl know you, then?" he asked at last.

"Is it literally true that she is going to the Château de Chillon with you?"

"I think that she fully intends it."

"Then, my dear Frederick," said Mrs. Costello, "I must decline the honor of her acquaintance. I am an old woman, but I am not too old, thank Heaven, to be shocked!"

"But don't they all do these things—the young girls in America?" Winterbourne inquired.

Mrs. Costello stared a moment. "I should like to see my granddaughters do them!" she declared, grimly.

This seemed to throw some light upon the matter, for Winterbourne remembered to have heard that his pretty cousins in New York were "tremendous flirts." If, therefore, Miss Daisy Miller exceeded the liberal margin allowed to these young ladies, it was probable that anything might be expected of her. Winterbourne was impatient to see her again, and he was vexed with himself that, by instinct, he should not appreciate her justly.

Though he was impatient to see her, he hardly knew what he should say to her about his aunt's refusal to become acquainted with her; but he discovered, promptly

enough, that with Miss Daisy Miller there was no grea
need of walking on tiptoe. He found her that evening i
the garden, wandering about in the warm starlight lik
an indolent sylph, and swinging to and fro the larges
fan he had ever beheld. It was ten o'clock. He had jus
dined with his aunt, had been sitting with her since din
ner, and had just taken leave of her till the morrow. Mis
Daisy Miller seemed very glad to see him; she declared i
was the longest evening she had ever passed.

"Have you been all alone?" he asked.

"I have been walking round with mother. But mothe
gets tired walking round," she answered.

"Has she gone to bed?"

"No; she doesn't like to go to bed," said the young
girl. "She doesn't sleep—not three hours. She says sh
doesn't know how she lives. She's dreadfully nervous.
guess she sleeps more than she thinks. She's gone some
where after Randolph; she wants to try to get him to g
to bed. He doesn't like to go to bed."

"Let us hope she will persuade him," observed Winter
bourne.

"She will talk to him all she can; but he doesn't lik
her to talk to him," said Miss Daisy, opening her fan
"She's going to try to get Eugenio to talk to him. Bu
he isn't afraid of Eugenio. Eugenio's a splendid courier
but he can't make much impression on Randolph! I don'
believe he'll go to bed before eleven." It appeared tha
Randolph's vigil was in fact triumphantly prolonged, fo
Winterbourne strolled about with the young girl fo
some time without meeting her mother. "I have bee
looking round for that lady you want to introduce me to,
his companion resumed. "She's your aunt." Then, o
Winterbourne's admitting the fact, and expressing som
curiosity as to how she had learned it, she said she ha
heard all about Mrs. Costello from the chambermaid. Sh
was very quiet, and very *comme il faut;* she wore whit
puffs; she spoke to no one, and she never dined at th
table d'hôte. Every two days she had a headache. "I thin

at's a lovely description, headache and all!" said Miss
Daisy, chattering along in her thin, gay voice. "I want to
ow her ever so much. I know just what *your* aunt would
; I know I should like her. She would be very exclusive.
ike a lady to be exclusive; I'm dying to be exclusive my-
f. Well, we *are* exclusive, mother and I. We don't speak
every one—or they don't speak to us. I suppose it's about
e same thing. Anyway, I shall be ever so glad to know
ur aunt."

Winterbourne was embarrassed. "She would be most
ppy," he said; "but I am afraid those headaches will
terfere."

The young girl looked at him through the dusk. "But
uppose she doesn't have a headache every day," she said,
npathetically.

Winterbourne was silent a moment. "She tells me she
es," he answered at last, not knowing what to say.

Miss Daisy Miller stopped, and stood looking at him.
r prettiness was still visible in the darkness; she was
ening and closing her enormous fan. "She doesn't want
know me!" she said, suddenly. "Why don't you say
You needn't be afraid. I'm not afraid!" And she gave a
tle laugh.

Winterbourne fancied there was a tremor in her voice;
was touched, shocked, mortified by it. "My dear young
ly," he protested, "she knows no one. It's her wretched
alth."

The young girl walked on a few steps, laughing still.
ou needn't be afraid," she repeated. "Why should she
nt to know me?" Then she paused again; she was close
the parapet of the garden, and in front of her was the
rlit lake. There was a vague sheen upon its surface,
d in the distance were dimly-seen mountain forms.
isy Miller looked out upon the mysterious prospect,
d then she gave another little laugh. "Gracious! she *is*
clusive!" she said. Winterbourne wondered whether
e was seriously wounded, and for a moment almost
shed that her sense of injury might be such as to make

it becoming in him to attempt to reassure and comfort h
He had a pleasant sense that she would be very approa
able for consolatory purposes. He felt then, for the
stant, quite ready to sacrifice his aunt, conversational
to admit that she was a proud, rude woman, and to
clare that they needn't mind her. But before he had ti
to commit himself to this perilous mixture of gallan
and impiety, the young lady, resuming her walk, gave
exclamation in quite another tone. "Well, here's moth
I guess she hasn't got Randolph to go to bed." The figu
of a lady appeared, at a distance, very indistinct in
darkness, and advancing with a slow and wavering mo
ment. Suddenly it seemed to pause.

"Are you sure it is your mother? Can you distingu
her in this thick dusk?" Winterbourne asked.

"Well!" cried Miss Daisy Miller, with a laugh; "I gu
I know my own mother. And when she has got on
shawl, too! She is always wearing my things."

The lady in question, ceasing to advance, hover
vaguely about the spot at which she had checked her ste

"I am afraid your mother doesn't see you," said Wint
bourne. "Or perhaps," he added, thinking, with M
Miller, the joke permissible—"perhaps she feels gui
about your shawl."

"Oh, it's a fearful old thing!" the young girl repli
serenely. "I told her she could wear it. She won't co
here, because she sees you."

"Ah, then," said Winterbourne, "I had better lea
you."

"Oh, no; come on!" urged Miss Daisy Miller.

"I'm afraid your mother doesn't approve of my wa
ing with you."

Miss Miller gave him a serious glance. "It isn't
me; it's for you—that is, it's for *her*. Well, I don't kn
who it's for! But mother doesn't like any of my gent
men friends. She's right down timid. She always ma
a fuss if I introduce a gentleman. But I *do* introd
them—almost always. If I didn't introduce my gent

146

en friends to mother," the young girl added, in her
tle soft, flat monotone, "I shouldn't think it was natural."
"To introduce me," said Winterbourne, "you must
ow my name." And he proceeded to pronounce it to her.
"Oh, dear, I can't say all that!" said his companion
ith a laugh. But by this time they had come up to Mrs.
iller, who, as they drew near, walked to the parapet of
e garden and leaned upon it, looking intently at the lake,
d turning her back to them. "Mother!" said the young
rl, in a tone of decision. Upon this the elder lady turned
und. "Mr. Winterbourne," said Miss Daisy Miller, in-
oducing the young man very frankly and prettily. "Com-
on," she was, as Mrs. Costello had pronounced her; yet
was a wonder to Winterbourne that, with her common-
ss, she had a singularly delicate grace.

Her mother was a small, spare, light person, with a
andering eye, a very exiguous nose, and a large fore-
ad, decorated with a certain amount of thin, much-
zzled hair. Like her daughter, Mrs. Miller was dressed
th extreme elegance; she had enormous diamonds in
r ears. So far as Winterbourne could observe, she gave
m no greeting—she certainly was not looking at him.
aisy was near her, pulling her shawl straight. "What are
u doing, poking round here?" this young lady in-
uired, but by no means with that harshness of accent
hich her choice of words may imply.

"I don't know," said her mother, turning toward the
ke again.

"I shouldn't think you'd want that shawl!" Daisy ex-
aimed.

"Well, I do!" her mother answered, with a little laugh.

"Did you get Randolph to go to bed?" asked the young
rl.

"No; I couldn't induce him," said Mrs. Miller, very
ntly. "He wants to talk to the waiter. He likes to talk
that waiter."

"I was telling Mr. Winterbourne," the young girl went
; and to the young man's ear her tone might have

indicated that she had been uttering his name all her li

"Oh yes!" said Winterbourne; "I have the pleasure
knowing your son."

Randolph's mamma was silent; she turned her attentic
to the lake. But at last she spoke. "Well, I don't see how
lives!"

"Anyhow, it isn't so bad as it was at Dover," said Dai
Miller.

"And what occurred at Dover?" Winterbourne asked.

"He wouldn't go to bed at all. I guess he sat up all nig
in the public parlor. He wasn't in bed at twelve o'cloc
I know that."

"It was half-past twelve," declared Mrs. Miller, wi
mild emphasis.

"Does he sleep much during the day?" Winterbour
demanded.

"I guess he doesn't sleep much," Daisy rejoined.

"I wish he would!" said her mother. "It seems as
he couldn't."

"I think he's real tiresome," Daisy pursued.

Then for some moments there was silence. "Well, Dai
Miller," said the elder lady, presently, "I shouldn't thir
you'd want to talk against your own brother!"

"Well, he *is* tiresome, mother," said Daisy, quite wi
out the asperity of a retort.

"He's only nine," urged Mrs. Miller.

"Well, he wouldn't go to that castle," said the you
girl. "I'm going there with Mr. Winterbourne."

To this announcement, very placidly made, Dais
mamma offered no response. Winterbourne took f
granted that she deeply disapproved of the project
excursion; but he said to himself that she was a simp
easily-managed person, and that a few deferential p
testations would take the edge from her displeasure. "Ye
he began; "your daughter has kindly allowed me t
honor of being her guide."

Mrs. Miller's wandering eyes attached themselves, wi
a sort of appealing air, to Daisy, who, however, stroll

few steps farther, gently humming to herself. "I preme you will go in the cars," said her mother.

"Yes, or in the boat," said Winterbourne.

"Well, of course, I don't know," Mrs. Miller rejoined. have never been to that castle."

"It is a pity you shouldn't go," said Winterbourne, beming to feel reassured as to her opposition. And yet was quite prepared to find that, as a matter of course, e meant to accompany her daughter.

"We've been thinking ever so much about going," she rsued; "but it seems as if we couldn't. Of course Daisy, e wants to go round. But there's a lady here—I don't ow her name—she says she shouldn't think we'd want go to see castles *here;* she should think we'd want to it till we got to Italy. It seems as if there would be so iny there," continued Mrs. Miller, with an air of in-easing confidence. "Of course we only want to see the incipal ones. We visited several in England," she pres-tly added.

"Ah, yes! in England there are beautiful castles," said interbourne. "But Chillon, here, is very well worth ing."

"Well, if Daisy feels up to it—" said Mrs. Miller, in a ie impregnated with a sense of the magnitude of the terprise. "It seems as if there was nothing she wouldn't dertake."

"Oh, I think she'll enjoy it!" Winterbourne declared. id he desired more and more to make it a certainty that was to have the privilege of a tête-à-tête with the young ly, who was still strolling along in front of them, softly calizing. "You are not disposed, madam," he inquired, undertake it yourself?"

Daisy's mother looked at him an instant askance, and en walked forward in silence. Then—"I guess she had tter go alone," she said, simply. Winterbourne observed himself that this was a very different type of maternity m that of the vigilant matrons who massed themselves the fore-front of social intercourse in the dark old city

at the other end of the lake. But his meditations were in
terrupted by hearing his name very distinctly pronounc
by Mrs. Miller's unprotected daughter.

"Mr. Winterbourne!" murmured Daisy.

"Mademoiselle!" said the young man.

"Don't you want to take me out in a boat?"

"At present?" he asked.

"Of course!" said Daisy.

"Well, Annie Miller!" exclaimed her mother.

"I beg you, madam, to let her go," said Winterbourn
ardently; for he had never yet enjoyed the sensation
guiding through the summer starlight a skiff freight
with a fresh and beautiful young girl.

"I shouldn't think she'd want to," said her mothe
"I should think she'd rather go indoors."

"I'm sure Mr. Winterbourne wants to take me," Dai
declared. "He's so awfully devoted!"

"I will row you over to Chillon in the starlight."

"I don't believe it!" said Daisy.

"Well!" ejaculated the elder lady again.

"You haven't spoken to me for half an hour," h
daughter went on.

"I have been having some very pleasant conversati
with your mother," said Winterbourne.

"Well, I want you to take me out in a boat!" Daisy
peated. They had all stopped, and she had turned rou
and was looking at Winterbourne. Her face wore a char
ing smile, her pretty eyes were gleaming, she was swingi
her great fan about. No; it's impossible to be prettier th
that, thought Winterbourne.

"There are half a dozen boats moored at that landi
place," he said, pointing to certain steps which descend
from the garden to the lake. "If you will do me the hon
to accept my arm, we will go and select one of them."

Daisy stood there smiling; she threw back her he
and gave a little light laugh. "I like a gentleman to
formal!" she declared.

"I assure you it's a formal offer."

"I was bound I would make you say something," Daisy
ent on.

"You see, it's not very difficult," said Winterbourne.
But I am afraid you are chaffing me."

"I think not, sir," remarked Mrs. Miller, very gently.

"Do, then, let me give you a row," he said to the young
rl.

"It's quite lovely, the way you say that!" cried Daisy.

"It will be still more lovely to do it."

"Yes, it would be lovely!" said Daisy. But she made no
ovement to accompany him; she only stood there laugh-
g.

"I should think you had better find out what time it
," interposed her mother.

"It is eleven o'clock, madam," said a voice, with a foreign
cent, out of the neighboring darkness; and Winter-
ourne, turning, perceived the florid personage who was
attendance upon the two ladies. He had apparently
st approached.

"Oh, Eugenio," said Daisy, "I am going out in a boat!"

Eugenio bowed. "At eleven o'clock, mademoiselle?"

"I am going with Mr. Winterbourne—this very minute."

"Do tell her she can't," said Mrs. Miller to the courier.

"I think you had better not go out in a boat, made-
oiselle," Eugenio declared.

Winterbourne wished to Heaven this pretty girl were
ot so familiar with her courier; but he said nothing.

"I suppose you don't think it's proper!" Daisy exclaimed.
Eugenio doesn't think anything's proper."

"I am at your service," said Winterbourne.

"Does mademoiselle propose to go alone?" asked Eu-
nio of Mrs. Miller.

"Oh, no; with this gentleman!" answered Daisy's
amma.

The courier looked for a moment at Winterbourne—
e latter thought he was smiling—and then, solemnly,
ith a bow, "As mademoiselle pleases!" he said.

"Oh, I hoped you would make a fuss!" said Daisy. "I

don't care to go now."

"I myself shall make a fuss if you don't go," said Win
terbourne.

"That's all I want—a little fuss!" And the young gi
began to laugh again.

"Mr. Randolph has gone to bed!" the courier an
nounced, frigidly.

"Oh, Daisy; now we can go!" said Mrs. Miller.

Daisy turned away from Winterbourne, looking at hin
smiling, and fanning herself. "Good-night," she said; "
hope you are disappointed, or disgusted, or something!"

He looked at her, taking the hand she offered him. "I an
puzzled," he answered.

"Well, I hope it won't keep you awake!" she said, ver
smartly; and, under the escort of the privileged Eugeni
the two ladies passed towards the house.

Winterbourne stood looking after them; he was indee
puzzled. He lingered beside the lake for a quarter of a
hour, turning over the mystery of the young girl's sudde
familiarities and caprices. But the only very definite co
clusion he came to was that he should enjoy deuced
"going off" with her somewhere.

Two days afterwards he went off with her to the Cast
of Chillon. He waited for her in the large hall of the hote
where the couriers, the servants, the foreign tourists, we
lounging about and staring. It was not the place he shou
have chosen, but she had appointed it. She came trippin
down-stairs, buttoning her long gloves, squeezing h
folded parasol against her pretty figure, dressed in the pe
fection of a soberly elegant travelling costume. Winte
bourne was a man of imagination and, as our ancesto
used to say, sensibility; as he looked at her dress and—c
the great staircase—her little rapid, confiding step, he fe
as if there were something romantic going forward. H
could have believed he was going to elope with her. H
passed out with her among all the idle people that a
sembled there; they were all looking at her very hard; sl
had begun to chatter as soon as she joined him. Winte

ourne's preference had been that they should be conveyed
o Chillon in a carriage; but she expressed a lively wish
o go in the little steamer; she declared that she had a
assion for steamboats. There was always such a lovely
reeze upon the water, and you saw such lots of people.
The sail was not long, but Winterbourne's companion
ound time to say a great many things. To the young man
imself their little excursion was so much of an escapade—
a adventure—that, even allowing for her habitual sense
f freedom, he had some expectation of seeing her regard
in the same way. But it must be confessed that, in this
articular, he was disappointed. Daisy Miller was ex-
remely animated, she was in charming spirits; but she was
pparently not at all excited; she was not fluttered; she
voided neither his eyes nor those of any one else; she
lushed neither when she looked at him nor when she
elt that people were looking at her. People continued
o look at her a great deal, and Winterbourne took much
atisfaction in his pretty companion's distinguished air.
Ie had been a little afraid that she would talk loud, laugh
vermuch, and even, perhaps, desire to move about the
oat a good deal. But he quite forgot his fears; he sat
miling, with his eyes upon her face, while, without mov-
ng from her place, she delivered herself of a great num-
er of original reflections. It was the most charming gar-
ulity he had ever heard. He had assented to the idea that
ae was "common"; but was she so, after all, or was he
mply getting used to her commonness? Her conversation
as chiefly of what metaphysicians term the objective cast;
ut every now and then it took a subjective turn.

"What on *earth* are you so grave about?" she suddenly
emanded, fixing her agreeable eyes upon Winterbourne's.

"Am I grave?" he asked. "I had an idea I was grinning
om ear to ear."

"You look as if you were taking me to a funeral. If that's
grin, your ears are very near together."

"Should you like me to dance a hornpipe on the deck?"

"Pray do, and I'll carry round your hat. It will pay the

expenses of our journey."

"I never was better pleased in my life," murmured Wi
terbourne.

She looked at him a moment, and then burst into
little laugh. "I like to make you say those things! You'
a queer mixture!"

In the castle, after they had landed, the subjective el
ment decidedly prevailed. Daisy tripped about the vaulte
chambers, rustled her skirts in the corkscrew staircase
flirted back with a pretty little cry and a shudder fro
the edge of the *oubliettes,* and turned a singularly wel
shaped ear to everything that Winterbourne told her abou
the place. But he saw that she cared very little for feud
antiquities, and that the dusky traditions of Chillon mac
but a slight impression upon her. They had the goo
fortune to have been able to walk about without oth
companionship than that of the custodian; and Winte
bourne arranged with this functionary—that they shou
not be hurried—that they should linger and pause wher
ever they chose. The custodian interpreted the barga
generously—Winterbourne, on his side, had been genero
—and ended by leaving them quite to themselves. Mi
Miller's observations were not remarkable for logical co
sistency; for anything she wanted to say she was sure
find a pretext. She found a great many pretexts in th
rugged embrasures of Chillon for asking Winterbour
sudden questions about himself—his family, his previo
history, his tastes, his habits, his intentions—and f
supplying information upon corresponding points in h
own personality. Of her own tastes, habits, and intentio
Miss Miller was prepared to give the most definite, an
indeed, the most favorable account.

"Well, I hope you know enough!" she said to her co
panion, after he had told her the history of the unhap
Bonnivard. "I never saw a man that knew so much!" T
history of Bonnivard had evidently, as they say, gone in
one ear and out of the other. But Daisy went on to sa
that she wished Winterbourne would travel with the

d "go round" with them; they might know something,
that case. "Don't you want to come and teach Ran-
lph?" she asked. Winterbourne said that nothing could
ssibly please him so much, but that he had unfortu-
tely other occupations. "Other occupations? I don't be-
ve it!" said Miss Daisy. "What do you mean? You are not
business." The young man admitted that he was not in
siness; but he had engagements which, even within a
y or two, would force him to go back to Geneva. "Oh,
ther!" she said; "I don't believe it!" and she began to
lk about something else. But a few moments later, when
was pointing out to her the pretty design of an antique
eplace, she broke out irrelevantly, "You don't mean to
y you are going back to Geneva?"

"It is a melancholy fact that I shall have to return to-
orrow."

"Well, Mr. Winterbourne," said Daisy, "I think you're
rrid!"

"Oh, don't say such dreadful things!" said Winter-
urne—"just at the last!"

"The last!" cried the young girl; "I call it the first.
have half a mind to leave you here and go straight back
the hotel alone." And for the next ten minutes she
d nothing but call him horrid. Poor Winterbourne was
rly bewildered; no young lady had as yet done him
e honor to be so agitated by the announcement of his
ovements. His companion, after this, ceased to pay any
tention to the curiosities of Chillon or the beauties of
e lake; she opened fire upon the mysterious charmer of
neva, whom she appeared to have instantly taken it
r granted that he was hurrying back to see. How did
iss Daisy Miller know that there was a charmer in
neva? Winterbourne, who denied the existence of such
person, was quite unable to discover; and he was di-
ded between amazement at the rapidity of her induc-
on and amusement at the frankness of her *persiflage*. She
emed to him, in all this, an extraordinary mixture of
nocence and crudity. "Does she never allow you more

than three days at a time?" asked Daisy, ironical
"Doesn't she give you a vacation in summer? There is
one so hard worked but they can get leave to go off som
where at this season. I suppose, if you stay another d:
she'll come after you in the boat. Do wait over till Frid:
and I will go down to the landing to see her arrive!" W
terbourne began to think he had been wrong to feel d
appointed in the temper in which the young lady h
embarked. If he had missed the personal accent, the p
sonal accent was now making its appearance. It sound
very distinctly, at last, in her telling him she would st
"teasing" him if he would promise her solemnly to co
down to Rome in the winter.

"That's not a difficult promise to make," said Wint
bourne. "My aunt has taken an apartment in Rome f
the winter, and has already asked me to come and see he:

"I don't want you to come for your aunt," said Dais
"I want you to come for me." And this was the or
allusion that the young man was ever to hear her ma
to his invidious kinswoman. He declared that, at a
rate, he would certainly come. After this Daisy stopp
teasing. Winterbourne took a carriage, and they dro
back to Vevay in the dusk. The young girl was very qui

In the evening Winterbourne mentioned to Mrs. C
tello that he had spent the afternoon at Chillon with M
Daisy Miller.

"The Americans—of the courier?" asked this lady.

"Ah, happily," said Winterbourne, "the courier stay
at home."

"She went with you all alone?"

"All alone."

Mrs. Costello sniffed a little at her smelling-bott
"And that," she exclaimed, "is the young person who
you wanted me to know!"

Rome

WINTERBOURNE, who had returned to Geneva the day after his excursion to Chillon, went to Rome towards the end of January. His aunt had been established there for several weeks, and he had received a couple of letters from her. "Those people you were so devoted to last summer at Vevay have turned up here, courier and all," she wrote. "They seem to have made several acquaintances, but the courier continues to be the most *intime*. The young lady, however, is also very intimate with some third-rate Italians, with whom she rackets about in a way that makes much talk. Bring me that pretty novel of Cherbuliez's—*Paule Méré*—and don't come later than the 23rd."

In the natural course of events, Winterbourne, on arriving in Rome, would presently have ascertained Mrs. Miller's address at the American banker's, and have gone to pay his compliments to Miss Daisy. "After what happened at Vevay, I think I may certainly call upon them," he said to Mrs. Costello.

"If, after what happens—at Vevay and everywhere—you desire to keep up the acquaintance, you are very welcome. Of course a man may know every one. Men are welcome to the privilege!"

"Pray, what is it that happens—here, for instance?" Winterbourne demanded.

"The girl goes about alone with her foreigners. As to what happens further, you must apply elsewhere for information. She has picked up half a dozen of the regular Roman fortune-hunters, and she takes them about to people's houses. When she comes to a party she brings with her a gentleman with a good deal of manner and a wonderful mustache."

"And where is the mother?"

"I haven't the least idea. They are very dreadful people

Winterbourne meditated a moment. "They are ve ignorant—very innocent only. Depend upon it they a not bad."

"They are hopelessly vulgar," said Mrs. Costel "Whether or no being hopelessly vulgar is being 'bad' a question for the metaphysicians. They are bad enou to dislike, at any rate; and for this short life that is qu enough."

The news that Daisy Miller was surrounded by half dozen wonderful mustaches checked Winterbourne's i pulse to go straightway to see her. He had, perhaps, n definitely flattered himself that he had made an ineffa able impression upon her heart, but he was annoyed hearing of a state of affairs so little in harmony with image that had lately flitted in and out of his own me tations; the image of a very pretty girl looking out of old Roman window and asking herself urgently when M Winterbourne would arrive. If, however, he determin to wait a little before reminding Miss Miller of his clai to her consideration, he went very soon to call upon tv or three other friends. One of these friends was an Ame can lady who had spent several winters at Geneva, whe she had placed her children at school. She was a very a complished woman, and she lived in the Via Gregorian Winterbourne found her in a little crimson drawing-roo on a third floor; the room was filled with southern su shine. He had not been there ten minutes when the ser ant came in, announcing "Madame Mila!" This announ ment was presently followed by the entrance of little Ra dolph Miller, who stopped in the middle of the room a stood staring at Winterbourne. An instant later his pre sister crossed the threshold; and then, after a consid able interval, Mrs. Miller slowly advanced.

"I know you!" said Randolph.

"I'm sure you know a great many things," exclaim Winterbourne, taking him by the hand. "How is yo lucation coming on?"

Daisy was exchanging greetings very prettily with her
ostess; but when she heard Winterbourne's voice she
uickly turned her head. "Well, I declare!" she said.

"I told you I should come, you know," Winterbourne
joined, smiling.

"Well, I didn't believe it," said Miss Daisy.

"I am much obliged to you," laughed the young man.

"You might have come to see me!" said Daisy.

"I arrived only yesterday."

"I don't believe that!" the young girl declared.

Winterbourne turned with a protesting smile to her
other; but this lady evaded his glance, and, seating her-
lf, fixed her eyes upon her son. "We've got a bigger place
an this," said Randolph. "It's all gold on the walls."

Mrs. Miller turned uneasily in her chair. "I told you
I were to bring you, you would say something!" she
urmured.

"I told *you!*" Randolph exclaimed. "I tell *you,* sir!"
e added, jocosely, giving Winterbourne a thump on the
ee. "It *is* bigger, too!"

Daisy had entered upon a lively conversation with her
ostess, and Winterbourne judged it becoming to address
few words to her mother. "I hope you have been well
nce we parted at Vevay," he said.

Mrs. Miller now certainly looked at him—at his chin.
Not very well, sir," she answered.

"She's got the dyspepsia," said Randolph. "I've got it,
o. Father's got it. I've got it most!"

This announcement, instead of embarrassing Mrs. Mil-
r, seemed to relieve her. "I suffer from the liver," she
id. "I think it's this climate; it's less bracing than Sche-
ectady, especially in the winter season. I don't know
hether you know we reside at Schenectady. I was saying
Daisy that I certainly hadn't found any one like Dr.
avis, and I didn't believe I should. Oh, at Schenectady
e stands first; they think everything of him. He has so
uch to do, and yet there was nothing he wouldn't do for

me. He said he never saw anything like my dyspepsia, b
he was bound to cure it. I'm sure there was nothing h
wouldn't try. He was just going to try something new whe
we came off. Mr. Miller wanted Daisy to see Europe f
herself. But I wrote to Mr. Miller that it seems as if
couldn't get on without Dr. Davis. At Schenectady h
stands at the very top; and there's a great deal of sickne
there, too. It affects my sleep."

Winterbourne had a good deal of pathological goss
with Dr. Davis's patient, during which Daisy chatted u
remittingly to her own companion. The young man aske
Mrs. Miller how she was pleased with Rome. "Well,
must say I am disappointed," she answered. "We had hea
so much about it; I suppose we had heard too much. B
we couldn't help that. We had been led to expect som
thing different."

"Ah, wait a little, and you will become very fond of it
said Winterbourne.

"I hate it worse and worse every day!" cried Randolp

"You are like the infant Hannibal," said Winterbourn

"No, I ain't!" Randolph declared, at a venture.

"You are not much like an infant," said his mothe
"But we have seen places," she resumed, "that I shou
put a long way before Rome." And in reply to Winte
bourne's interrogation, "There's Zürich," she conclude
"I think Zürich is lovely; and we hadn't heard half
much about it."

"The best place we've seen is the City of Richmond,
said Randolph.

"He means the ship," his mother explained. "We crosse
in that ship. Randolph had a good time on the *City
Richmond*."

"It's the best place I've seen," the child repeated. "On
it was turned the wrong way."

"Well, we've got to turn the right way some time," sai
Mrs. Miller, with a little laugh. Winterbourne expresse
the hope that her daughter at least found some gratifica
tion in Rome, and she declared that Daisy was quite ca

ried away. "It's on account of the society—the society's splendid. She goes round everywhere; she has made a great number of acquaintances. Of course she goes round more than I do. I must say they have been very sociable; they have taken her right in. And then she knows a great many gentlemen. Oh, she thinks there's nothing like Rome. Of course, it's a great deal pleasanter for a young lady if she knows plenty of gentlemen."

By this time Daisy had turned her attention again to Winterbourne. "I've been telling Mrs. Walker how mean you were!" the young girl announced.

"And what is the evidence you have offered?" asked Winterbourne, rather annoyed at Miss Miller's want of appreciation of the zeal of an admirer who on his way down to Rome had stopped neither at Bologna nor at Florence, simply because of a certain sentimental impatience. He remembered that a cynical compatriot had once told him that American women—the pretty ones, and this gave a largeness to the axiom—were at once the most exacting in the world and the least endowed with a sense of indebtedness.

"Why, you were awfully mean at Vevay," said Daisy. "You wouldn't do anything. You wouldn't stay there when I asked you."

"My dearest young lady," cried Winterbourne, with eloquence, "have I come all the way to Rome to encounter your reproaches?"

"Just hear him say that!" said Daisy to her hostess, giving a twist to a bow on this lady's dress. "Did you ever hear anything so quaint?"

"So quaint, my dear?" murmured Mrs. Walker, in the tone of a partisan of Winterbourne.

"Well, I don't know," said Daisy, fingering Mrs. Walker's ribbons. "Mrs. Walker, I want to tell you something."

"Mother-r," interposed Randolph, with his rough ends to his words, "I tell you you've got to go. Eugenio'll raise—something!"

"I'm not afraid of Eugenio," said Daisy, with a toss of

her head. "Look here, Mrs. Walker," she went on, "yo
know I'm coming to your party."

"I am delighted to hear it."

"I've got a lovely dress!"

"I am very sure of that."

"But I want to ask a favor—permission to bring
friend."

"I shall be happy to see any of your friends," said Mr
Walker, turning with a smile to Mrs. Miller.

"Oh, they are not my friends," answered Daisy's mamm
smiling shyly, in her own fashion. "I never spoke to them.

"It's an intimate friend of mine—Mr. Giovanelli," sai
Daisy, without a tremor in her clear little voice, or
shadow on her brilliant little face.

Mrs. Walker was silent a moment; she gave a rapi
glance at Winterbourne. "I shall be glad to see Mr. Gi
vanelli," she then said.

"He's an Italian," Daisy pursued with the prettie
serenity. "He's a great friend of mine; he's the handsome
man in the world—except Mr. Winterbourne! He know
plenty of Italians, but he wants to know some American
He thinks ever so much of Americans. He's tremendousl
clever. He's perfectly lovely!"

It was settled that this brilliant personage should b
brought to Mrs. Walker's party, and then Mrs. Miller pr
pared to take her leave. "I guess we'll go back to the hotel
she said.

"You may go back to the hotel, mother, but I'm goin
to take a walk," said Daisy.

"She's going to walk with Mr. Giovanelli," Randolp
proclaimed.

"I am going to the Pincio," said Daisy, smiling.

"Alone, my dear—at this hour?" Mrs. Walker asked. Th
afternoon was drawing to a close—it was the hour for th
throng of carriages and of contemplative pedestrians. "
don't think it's safe, my dear," said Mrs. Walker.

"Neither do I," subjoined Mrs. Miller. "You'll get th
fever, as sure as you live. Remember what Dr. Davis tol

162

you!"

"Give her some medicine before she goes," said Randolph.

The company had risen to its feet; Daisy, still showing her pretty teeth, bent over and kissed her hostess. "Mrs. Walker, you are too perfect," she said. "I'm not going alone; I am going to meet a friend."

"Your friend won't keep you from getting the fever," Mrs. Miller observed.

"Is it Mr. Giovanelli?" asked the hostess.

Winterbourne was watching the young girl; at this question his attention quickened. She stood there smiling and smoothing her bonnet ribbons; she glanced at Winterbourne. Then, while she glanced and smiled, she answered, without a shade of hesitation, "Mr. Giovanelli—the beautiful Giovanelli."

"My dear young friend," said Mrs. Walker, taking her hand, pleadingly, "don't walk off to the Pincio at this unhealthy hour to meet a beautiful Italian."

"Well, he speaks English," said Mrs. Miller.

"Gracious me!" Daisy exclaimed, "I don't want to do anything improper. There's an easy way to settle it." She continued to glance at Winterbourne. "The Pincio is only a hundred yards distant; and if Mr. Winterbourne were as polite as he pretends, he would offer to walk with me!"

Winterbourne's politeness hastened to affirm itself, and the young girl gave him gracious leave to accompany her. They passed down-stairs before her mother, and at the door Winterbourne perceived Mrs. Miller's carriage drawn up, with the ornamental courier whose acquaintance he had made at Vevay, seated within. "Good-bye, Eugenio!" cried Daisy; "I'm going to take a walk." The distance from the Via Gregoriana to the other end of the Pincian Hill is, in fact, rapidly traversed. As the day was splendid, however, and the concourse of vehicles, walkers, and loungers numerous, the young Americans found their progress much delayed. This fact was highly agreeable to Winterbourne, in spite of his consciousness of his singular situation. The slow-moving, idly-gazing Roman crowd bestowed much attention upon the extremely pretty young foreign lady who was passing through it upon his arm; and he wondered what on earth had been in Daisy's mind when she proposed to expose herself, unattended, to its appreciation. His own mission, to her sense, apparently, was to consign her to the hands of Mr. Giovanelli; but Winterbourne, at once annoyed and gratified, resolved that he would do no such thing.

"Why haven't you been to see me?" asked Daisy. "You can't get out of that."

"I have had the honor of telling you that I have only just stepped out of the train."

"You must have stayed in the train a good while after it stopped!" cried the young girl, with her little laugh. "I suppose you were asleep. You have had time to go to see Mrs. Walker."

"I knew Mrs. Walker—" Winterbourne began to explain.

"I know where you knew her. You knew her at Geneva. She told me so. Well, you knew me at Vevay. That's just as good. So you ought to have come." She asked him no other questions than this; she began to prattle about her own affairs. "We've got splendid rooms at the hotel; Eugenio says they're the best rooms in Rome. We are going to stay all winter, if we don't die of the fever; and I guess we'll stay then. It's a great deal nicer than I thought; I thought it would be fearfully quiet; I was sure it would be awfully poky. I was sure we should be going round all the time with one of those dreadful old men that explain about the pictures and things. But we only had about a week of that, and now I'm enjoying myself. I know ever so many people, and they are all so charming. The society's extremely select. There are all kinds—English and Germans and Italians. I think I like the English best. I like their style of conversation. But there are some lovely Americans. I never saw anything so hospitable.

here's something or other every day. There's not much
ncing; but I must say I never thought dancing was
erything. I was always fond of conversation. I guess I
all have plenty at Mrs. Walker's, her rooms are so
all." When they had passed the gate of the Pincian
ardens, Miss Miller began to wonder where Mr. Gio-
nelli might be. "We had better go straight to that place
front," she said, "where you look at the view."

"I certainly shall not help you to find him," Winter-
urne declared.

"Then I shall find him without you," said Miss Daisy.
She burst into her little laugh. "Are you afraid you'll
t lost—or run over? But there's Giovanelli, leaning
ainst that tree. He's staring at the women in the car-
ges; did you ever see anything so cool?"

Winterbourne perceived at some distance a little man
nding with folded arms nursing his cane. He had a
ndsome face, an artfully poised hat, a glass in one eye,
d a nosegay in his buttonhole. Winterbourne looked
him a moment, and then said, "Do you mean to speak
that man?"

"Do I mean to speak to him? Why, you don't suppose
mean to communicate by signs?"

"Pray understand, then," said Winterbourne, "that I
tend to remain with you."

Daisy stopped and looked at him, without a sign of
ubled consciousness in her face; with nothing but the
esence of her charming eyes and her happy dimples.
Vell, she's a cool one!" thought the young man.

"I don't like the way you say that," said Daisy. "It's too
perious."

"I beg your pardon if I say it wrong. The main point is
give you an idea of my meaning."

The young girl looked at him more gravely, but with
es that were prettier than ever. "I have never allowed
gentleman to dictate to me, or to interfere with anything
do."

"I think you have made a mistake," said Winterbourne.

"You should sometimes listen to a gentleman—the rig[ht]
one."

Daisy began to laugh again. "I do nothing but liste[n]
to gentlemen!" she exclaimed. "Tell me if Mr. Giov[a]-
nelli is the right one."

The gentleman with the nosegay in his bosom had no[w]
perceived our two friends, and was approaching the youn[g]
girl with obsequious rapidity. He bowed to Winterbourn[e]
as well as to the latter's companion; he had a brillian[t]
smile, an intelligent eye; Winterbourne thought him n[ot]
a bad-looking fellow. But he nevertheless said to Dais[y]
"No, he's not the right one."

Daisy evidently had a natural talent for performing i[n]-
troductions; she mentioned the name of each of her co[m]-
panions to the other. She strolled along with one of the[m]
on each side of her; Mr. Giovanelli, who spoke Engli[sh]
very cleverly—Winterbourne afterwards learned that [he]
had practised the idiom upon a great many America[n]
heiresses—addressed to her a great deal of very poli[te]
nonsense; he was extremely urbane, and the young Ame[r]-
ican, who said nothing, reflected upon that profundi[ty]
of Italian cleverness which enables people to appear mo[re]
gracious in proportion as they are more acutely disa[p]-
pointed. Giovanelli, of course, had counted upon som[e]-
thing more intimate; he had not bargained for a par[ty]
of three. But he kept his temper in a manner which su[g]-
gested far-stretching intentions. Winterbourne flatter[ed]
himself that he had taken his measure. "He is not a gent[le]-
man," said the young American; "he is only a clev[er]
imitation of one. He is a music-master, or a penny-a-lin[er,]
or a third-rate artist. D—n his good looks!" Mr. Giovane[lli]
had certainly a very pretty face; but Winterbourne f[elt]
a superior indignation at his own lovely fellow-count[ry]-
woman's not knowing the difference between a spurio[us]
gentleman and a real one. Giovanelli chattered and jeste[d]
and made himself wonderfully agreeable. It was true th[at]
if he was an imitation, the imitation was brilliant. "Nev[er-]
theless," Winterbourne said to himself, "a nice girl oug[ht]

o know!" And then he came back to the question whether his was, in fact, a nice girl. Would a nice girl, even allowing for her being a little American flirt, make a rendezvous with a presumably low-lived foreigner? The rendezvous in this case, indeed, had been in broad daylight, and in the most crowded corner of Rome; but was it not impossible to regard the choice of these circumstances as a proof of extreme cynicism? Singular though it may seem, Winterbourne was vexed that the young girl, in joining her *amoroso,* should not appear more impatient of his own company, and he was vexed because of his inclination. It was impossible to regard her as a perfectly well-conducted young lady; she was wanting in a certain indispensable delicacy. It would therefore simplify matters greatly to be able to treat her as the object of one of those sentiments which are called by romancers "lawless passions." That she should seem to wish to get rid of him would help him to think more lightly of her, and to be able to think more lightly of her would make her much less perplexing. But Daisy, on this occasion, continued to present herself as an inscrutable combination of audacity and innocence.

She had been walking some quarter of an hour, attended by her two cavaliers, and responding in a tone of very childish gayety, as it seemed to Winterbourne, to the pretty speeches of Mr. Giovanelli, when a carriage that had detached itself from the revolving train drew up beside the path. At the same moment Winterbourne perceived that his friend Mrs. Walker—the lady whose house he had lately left—was seated in the vehicle, and was beckoning to him. Leaving Miss Miller's side, he hastened to obey her summons. Mrs. Walker was flushed; she wore an excited air. "It is really too dreadful," she said. "That girl must not do this sort of thing. She must not walk here with you two men. Fifty people have noticed her."

Winterbourne raised his eyebrows. "I think it's a pity to make too much fuss about it."

"It's a pity to let the girl ruin herself."

"She is very innocent," said Winterbourne.

"She's very crazy!" cried Mrs. Walker. "Did you ever see anything so imbecile as her mother? After you had all left me just now I could not sit still for thinking of it. It seemed too pitiful not even to attempt to save her. I ordered the carriage and put on my bonnet, and came here as quickly as possible. Thank Heaven I have found you!"

"What do you propose to do with us?" asked Winterbourne, smiling.

"To ask her to get in, to drive her about here for half an hour, so that the world may see that she is not running absolutely wild, and then to take her safely home."

"I don't think it's a very happy thought," said Winterbourne; "but you can try."

Mrs. Walker tried. The young man went in pursuit of Miss Miller, who had simply nodded and smiled at his interlocutor in the carriage, and had gone her way with her companion. Daisy, on learning that Mrs. Walker wished to speak to her, retraced her steps with a perfect good grace and with Mr. Giovanelli at her side. She declared that she was delighted to have a chance to present this gentleman to Mrs. Walker. She immediately achieved the introduction, and declared that she had never in her life seen anything so lovely as Mrs. Walker's carriage-rug.

"I am glad you admire it," said this lady, smiling sweetly. "Will you get in and let me put it over you?"

"Oh no, thank you," said Daisy. "I shall admire it much more as I see you driving round with it."

"Do get in and drive with me!" said Mrs. Walker.

"That would be charming, but it's so enchanting just as I am!" and Daisy gave a brilliant glance at the gentlemen on either side of her.

"It may be enchanting, dear child, but it is not the custom here," urged Mrs. Walker, leaning forward in her victoria, with her hands devoutly clasped.

"Well, it ought to be, then!" said Daisy. "If I didn't

k I should expire."

You should walk with your mother, dear," cried the
v from Geneva, losing patience.

With my mother, dear!" exclaimed the young girl.
iterbourne saw that she scented interference. "My
her never walked ten steps in her life. And then, you
w," she added, with a laugh, "I am more than five
s old."

You are old enough to be more reasonable. You are
enough, dear Miss Miller, to be talked about."

aisy looked at Mrs. Walker, smiling intensely. "Talked
ut? What do you mean?"

Come into my carriage, and I will tell you."

aisy turned her quickened glance again from one of
gentlemen beside her to the other. Mr. Giovanelli was
ing to and fro, rubbing down his gloves and laughing
agreeably; Winterbourne thought it a most unpleas-
scene. "I don't think I want to know what you mean,"
Daisy, presently. "I don't think I should like it."

Winterbourne wished that Mrs. Walker would tuck in
carriage-rug and drive away; but this lady did not
oy being defied, as she afterwards told him. "Should
prefer being thought a very reckless girl?" she de-
ided.

Gracious!" exclaimed Daisy. She looked again at Mr.
vanelli, then she turned to Winterbourne. There was
ttle pink flush in her cheek; she was tremendously
ty. "Does Mr. Winterbourne think," she asked slowly,
ling, throwing back her head and glancing at him
n head to foot, "that, to save my reputation, I ought
et into the carriage?"

Winterbourne colored; for an instant he hesitated
itly. It seemed so strange to hear her speak that way
er "reputation." But he himself, in fact, must speak
iccordance with gallantry. The finest gallantry here
simply to tell her the truth, and the truth for Win-
ourne—as the few indications I have been able to
have made him known to the reader—was that Daisy

Miller should have taken Mrs. Walker's advice. He look
at her exquisite prettiness, and then said, very gently,
think you should get into the carriage."

Daisy gave a violent laugh. "I never heard anyth
so stiff! If this is improper, Mrs. Walker," she pursu
"then I am all improper, and you must give me up. Go
bye; I hope you'll have a lovely ride!" and, with Mr. C
vanelli, who made a triumphantly obsequious salute,
turned away.

Mrs. Walker sat looking after her, and there were te
in Mrs. Walker's eyes. "Get in here, sir," she said to W
terbourne, indicating the place beside her. The yo
man answered that he felt bound to accompany Miss M
ler; whereupon Mrs. Walker declared that if he refu
her this favor she would never speak to him again. She
evidently in earnest. Winterbourne overtook Daisy a
her companion, and, offering the young girl his ha
told her that Mrs. Walker had made an imperious cla
upon his society. He expected that in answer she wo
say something rather free, something to commit her
still further to that "recklessness" from which M
Walker had so charitably endeavored to dissuade her.
she only shook his hand, hardly looking at him; w
Mr. Giovanelli bade him farewell with a too empha
flourish of the hat.

Winterbourne was not in the best possible humor
he took his seat in Mrs. Walker's victoria. "That was
clever of you," he said, candidly, while the vehicle ming
again with the throng of carriages.

"In such a case," his companion answered, "I do
wish to be clever; I wish to be *earnest!*"

"Well, your earnestness has only offended her and
her off."

"It has happened very well," said Mrs. Walker.
she is so perfectly determined to compromise herself,
sooner one knows it the better; one can act according

"I suspect she meant no harm," Winterbourne rejoin

"So I thought a month ago. But she has been going

r."

"What has she been doing?"

"Everything that is not done here. Flirting with any
an she could pick up; sitting in corners with mysterious
alians; dancing all the evening with the same partners;
ceiving visits at eleven o'clock at night. Her mother
es away when visitors come."

"But her brother," said Winterbourne, laughing, "sits
till midnight."

"He must be edified by what he sees. I'm told that at
eir hotel every one is talking about her, and that a
nile goes round among all the servants when a gentle-
an comes and asks for Miss Miller."

"The servants be hanged!" said Winterbourne, angrily.
The poor girl's only fault," he presently added, "is that
e is very uncultivated."

"She is naturally indelicate," Mrs. Walker declared.
Take that example this morning. How long had you
nown her at Vevay?"

"A couple of days."

"Fancy, then, her making it a personal matter that you
ould have left the place?"

Winterbourne was silent for some moments; then he
id, "I suspect, Mrs. Walker, that you and I have lived
o long at Geneva!" And he added a request that she
ould inform him with what particular design she had
ade him enter the carriage.

"I wished to beg you to cease your relations with Miss
iller—not to flirt with her—to give her no further op-
ortunity to expose herself—to let her alone, in short."

"I'm afraid I can't do that," said Winterbourne. "I
ke her extremely."

"All the more reason that you shouldn't help her to
ake a scandal."

"There shall be nothing scandalous in my attentions
 her."

"There certainly will be in the way she takes them.
ut I have said what I had on my conscience," Mrs. Walker

pursued. "If you wish to rejoin the young lady I will pu
you down. Here, by-the-way, you have a chance."

The carriage was traversing that part of the Pincia
Garden that overhangs the wall of Rome and overlook
the beautiful Villa Borghese. It is bordered by a larg
parapet, near which there are several seats. One of th
seats at a distance was occupied by a gentleman and
lady, towards which Mrs. Walker gave a toss of her head
At the same moment these persons rose and walked to
wards the parapet. Winterbourne had asked the coach
man to stop; he now descended from the carriage. H
companion looked at him a moment in silence; then
while he raised his hat, she drove majestically away. Win
terbourne stood there; he had turned his eyes toward
Daisy and her cavalier. They evidently saw no one; the
were too deeply occupied with each other. When the
reached the low garden-wall they stood a moment lookin
off at the great flat-topped pine-clusters of the Villa Bo
ghese; then Giovanelli seated himself familiarly upon th
broad ledge of the wall. The western sun in the opposit
sky sent out a brilliant shaft through a couple of clou
bars, whereupon Daisy's companion took her parasol ou
of her hands and opened it. She came a little nearer, an
he held the parasol over her; then, still holding it, he le
it rest upon her shoulder, so that both of their heads wer
hidden from Winterbourne. This young man lingered
moment, then he began to walk. But he walked—no
towards the couple with the parasol—towards the res
dence of his aunt, Mrs. Costello.

He flattered himself on the following day that ther
was no smiling among the servants when he, at leas
asked for Mrs. Miller at her hotel. This lady and he
daughter, however, were not at home; and on the nex
day after, repeating his visit, Winterbourne again ha
the misfortune not to find them. Mrs. Walker's part
took place on the evening of the third day, and, in spite o
the frigidity of his last interview with the hostess, Winte
bourne was among the guests. Mrs. Walker was one o

ɔse American ladies who, while residing abroad, make
point, in their own phrase, of studying European so-
ty; and she had on this occasion collected several speci-
ɛns of her diversely-born fellow-mortals to serve, as it
re, as text-books. When Winterbourne arrived, Daisy
iller was not there, but in a few moments he saw her
ther come in alone, very shyly and ruefully. Mrs. Mil-
's hair above her exposed-looking temples was more
zzled than ever. As she approached Mrs. Walker, Win-
bourne also drew near.

"You see I've come all alone," said poor Mrs. Miller.
'm so frightened I don't know what to do. It's the first
ne I've ever been to a party alone, especially in this
untry. I wanted to bring Randolph, or Eugenio, or
ne one, but Daisy just pushed me off by myself. I ain't
ɛd to going round alone."

"And does not your daughter intend to favor us with
r society?" demanded Mrs. Walker, impressively.

"Well, Daisy's all dressed," said Mrs. Miller, with that
cent of the dispassionate, if not of the philosophic, his-
rian with which she always recorded incidents of her
ughter's career. "She got dressed on purpose before
ɪnner. But she's got a friend of hers there; that gentle-
ɪn—the Italian—that she wanted to bring. They've got
ing at the piano; it seems as if they couldn't leave off.
ɪ. Giovanelli sings splendidly. But I guess they'll come
fore very long," concluded Mrs. Miller, hopefully.

"I'm sorry she should come in that way," said Mrs.
alker.

"Well, I told her that there was no use in her getting
ɛssed before dinner if she was going to wait three hours,"
sponded Daisy's mamma. "I didn't see the use of her
ɪtting on such a dress as that to sit around with Mr. Gio-
nelli."

"This is most horrible!" said Mrs. Walker, turning
ay and addressing herself to Winterbourne. *"Elle
ffiche.* It's her revenge for my having ventured to re-
ɔnstrate with her. When she comes I shall not speak to

173

her."

Daisy came after eleven o'clock; but she was not, such an occasion, a young lady to wait to be spoken She rustled forward in radiant loveliness, smiling a chattering, carrying a large bouquet, and attended Mr. Giovanelli. Every one stopped talking, and turn and looked at her. She came straight to Mrs. Walker. "I afraid you thought I never was coming, so I sent moth off to tell you. I wanted to make Mr. Giovanelli pract some things before he came; you know he sings beau fully, and I want you to ask him to sing. This is Mr. G vanelli; you know I introduced him to you; he's got t most lovely voice, and he knows the most charming s of songs. I made him go over them this evening on pu pose; we had the greatest time at the hotel." Of all th Daisy delivered herself with the sweetest, brightest au bleness, looking now at her hostess and now round t room, while she gave a series of little pats round her sho ders to the edges of her dress. "Is there any one I know she asked.

"I think every one knows you!" said Mrs. Walker, pre nantly, and she gave a very cursory greeting to Mr. G vanelli. This gentleman bore himself gallantly. He smil and bowed, and showed his white teeth; he curled l mustaches and rolled his eyes, and performed all t proper functions of a handsome Italian at an eveni party. He sang very prettily half a dozen songs, thou Mrs. Walker afterwards declared that she had been qu unable to find out who asked him. It was apparently n Daisy who had given him his orders. Daisy sat at a d tance from the piano; and though she had publicly, as were, professed a high admiration for his singing, talke not inaudibly, while it was going on.

"It's a pity these rooms are so small; we can't dance she said to Winterbourne, as if she had seen him fi minutes before.

"I am not sorry we can't dance," Winterbourne a swered; "I don't dance."

"Of course you don't dance; you're too stiff," said Miss Daisy. "I hope you enjoyed your drive with Mrs. Walker."

"No, I didn't enjoy it; I preferred walking with you."

"We paired off; that was much better," said Daisy. "But did you ever hear anything so cool as Mrs. Walker's wanting me to get into her carriage and drop poor Mr. Giovanelli, and under the pretext that it was proper? People have different ideas! It would have been most unkind; he had been talking about that walk for ten days."

"He should not have talked about it at all," said Winterbourne; "he would never have proposed to a young lady of this country to walk about the streets with him."

"About the streets?" cried Daisy, with her pretty stare. "Where, then, would he have proposed to her to walk? The Pincio is not the streets, either; and I, thank goodness, am not a young lady of this country. The young ladies of this country have a dreadfully poky time of it, so far as I can learn; I don't see why I should change my habits for *them.*"

"I am afraid your habits are those of a flirt," said Winterbourne, gravely.

"Of course they are," she cried, giving him her little smiling stare again. "I'm a fearful, frightful flirt! Did you ever hear of a nice girl that was not? But I suppose you will tell me now that I am not a nice girl."

"You're a very nice girl; but I wish you would flirt with me, and me only," said Winterbourne.

"Ah! thank you—thank you very much; you are the last man I should think of flirting with. As I have had the pleasure of informing you, you are too stiff."

"You say that too often," said Winterbourne.

Daisy gave a delighted laugh. "If I could have the sweet hope of making you angry, I should say it again."

"Don't do that; when I am angry I'm stiffer than ever. But if you won't flirt with me, do cease, at least, to flirt with your friend at the piano; they don't understand that sort of thing here."

"I thought they understood nothing else!" exclaimed

Daisy.

"Not in young unmarried women."

"It seems to me much more proper in young unmarried women than in old married ones," Daisy declared.

"Well," said Winterbourne, "when you deal with na-
tives you must go by the custom of the place. Flirting
a purely American custom; it doesn't exist here. So wh
you show yourself in public with Mr. Giovanelli, a
without your mother—"

"Gracious! poor mother!" interposed Daisy.

"Though you may be flirting, Mr. Giovanelli is not;
means something else."

"He isn't preaching, at any rate," said Daisy, wi
vivacity. "And if you want very much to know, we are t
good friends for that: we are very intimate friends."

"Ah!" rejoined Winterbourne, "if you are in love wi
each other, it is another affair."

She had allowed him up to this point to talk so frank
that he had no expectation of shocking her by this ejac
lation; but she immediately got up, blushing visibly, a
leaving him to exclaim mentally that little Americ
flirts were the queerest creatures in the world. "Mr. G
vanelli, at least," she said, giving her interlocutor a sing
glance, "never says such very disagreeable things to me

Winterbourne was bewildered; he stood staring. M
Giovanelli had finished singing. He left the piano a
came over to Daisy. "Won't you come into the other roo
and have some tea?" he asked, bending before her wi
his ornamental smile.

Daisy turned to Winterbourne, beginning to sm
again. He was still more perplexed, for this inconseque
smile made nothing clear, though it seemed to pro
indeed, that she had a sweetness and softness that
verted instinctively to the pardon of offences. "It has nev
occurred to Mr. Winterbourne to offer me any tea," s
she said, with her little tormenting manner.

"I have offered you advice," Winterbourne rejoined.

"I prefer weak tea!" cried Daisy, and she went off wi

he brilliant Giovanelli. She sat with him in the adjoin-
ng room, in the embrasure of the window, for the rest
of the evening. There was an interesting performance
at the piano, but neither of these young people gave heed
to it. When Daisy came to take leave of Mrs. Walker, this
lady conscientiously repaired the weakness of which she
had been guilty at the moment of the young girl's arrival.
She turned her back straight upon Miss Miller, and left
her to depart with what grace she might. Winterbourne
was standing near the door; he saw it all. Daisy turned
very pale, and looked at her mother; but Mrs. Miller was
humbly unconscious of any violation of the usual social
norms. She appeared, indeed, to have felt an incongruous
impulse to draw attention to her own striking observance
of them. "Good-night, Mrs. Walker," she said; "we've had
a beautiful evening. You see, if I let Daisy come to parties
without me, I don't want her to go away without me."
Daisy turned away, looking with a pale, grave face at the
circle near the door; Winterbourne saw that, for the first
moment, she was too much shocked and puzzled even for
indignation. He on his side was greatly touched.

"That was very cruel," he said to Mrs. Walker.

"She never enters my drawing-room again!" replied
his hostess.

Since Winterbourne was not to meet her in Mrs. Walker's drawing-room, he went as often as possible to Mrs.
Miller's hotel. The ladies were rarely at home; but when
he found them the devoted Giovanelli was always present.
Very often the brilliant little Roman was in the drawing-
room with Daisy alone, Mrs. Miller being apparently
constantly of the opinion that discretion is the better part
of surveillance. Winterbourne noted, at first with surprise,
that Daisy on these occasions was never embarrassed or
annoyed by his own entrance; but he very presently began
to feel that she had no more surprises for him; the un-
expected in her behavior was the only thing to expect.
She showed no displeasure at her tête-à-tête with Giovanelli being interrupted; she could chatter as freshly and

freely with two gentlemen as with one; there was always
in her conversation, the same odd mixture of audacity and
puerility. Winterbourne remarked to himself that if she
was seriously interested in Giovanelli, it was very singular
that she should not take more trouble to preserve the
sanctity of their interviews; and he liked her the more for
her innocent-looking indifference and her apparently in-
exhaustible good-humor. He could hardly have said why,
but she seemed to him a girl who would never be jealous.
At the risk of exciting a somewhat derisive smile on the
reader's part, I may affirm that with regard to the women
who had hitherto interested him, it very often seemed to
Winterbourne among the possibilities that, given certain
contingencies, he should be afraid—literally afraid—of
these ladies; he had a pleasant sense that he should never
be afraid of Daisy Miller. It must be added that this sentiment was not altogether flattering to Daisy; it was part of
his conviction, or rather of his apprehension, that she
would prove a very light young person.

But she was evidently very much interested in Giovanelli. She looked at him whenever he spoke; she was
perpetually telling him to do this and to do that; she was
constantly "chaffing" and abusing him. She appeared
completely to have forgotten that Winterbourne had said
anything to displease her at Mrs. Walker's little party. One
Sunday afternoon, having gone to St. Peter's with his
aunt, Winterbourne perceived Daisy strolling about the
great church in company with the inevitable Giovanelli.
Presently he pointed out the young girl and her cavalier
to Mrs. Costello. This lady looked at them a moment
through her eye-glass, and then she said,

"That's what makes you so pensive in these days, eh?"

"I had not the least idea I was pensive," said the young
man.

"You are very much preoccupied; you are thinking of
something."

"And what is it," he asked, "that you accuse me of
thinking of?"

"Oh that young lady's—Miss Baker's, Miss Chandler's —what's her name?—Miss Miller's intrigue with that little barber's block."

"Do you call it an intrigue," Winterbourne asked— an affair that goes on with such peculiar publicity?"

"That's their folly," said Mrs. Costello; "it's not their merit."

"No," rejoined Winterbourne, with something of that pensiveness to which his aunt had alluded. "I don't believe that there is anything to be called an intrigue."

"I have heard a dozen people speak of it; they say she s quite carried away by him."

"They're certainly very intimate," said Winterbourne. Mrs. Costello inspected the young couple again with her optical instrument. "He is very handsome. One easily sees how it is. She thinks him the most elegant man in the world—the finest gentleman. She has never seen anything like him; he is better, even, than the courier. It was the courier, probably, who introduced him; and if he succeeds in marrying the young lady, the courier will come in for a magnificent commission."

"I don't believe she thinks of marrying him," said Winterbourne, "and I don't believe he hopes to marry her."

"You may be very sure she thinks of nothing. She goes on from day to day, from hour to hour, as they did in the Golden Age. I can imagine nothing more vulgar. And at the same time," added Mrs. Costello, "depend upon it that she may tell you any moment that she is 'engaged.'"

"I think that is more than Giovanelli expects," said Winterbourne.

"Who is Giovanelli?"

"The little Italian. I have asked questions about him, and learned something. He is apparently a perfectly respectable little man. I believe he is, in a small way, a *cavaliere avvocato*. But he doesn't move in what are called the first circles. I think it is really not absolutely impossible that the courier introduced him. He is evidently immensely charmed with Miss Miller. If she thinks him the

finest gentleman in the world, he, on his side, has neve
found himself in personal contact with such splendor
such opulence, such expensiveness, as this young lady's
And then she must seem to him wonderfully pretty and
interesting. I rather doubt that he dreams of marrying
her. That must appear to him too impossible a piece o
luck. He has nothing but his handsome face to offer, and
there is a substantial Mr. Miller in that mysterious land
of dollars. Giovanelli knows that he hasn't a title to offer
If he were only a count or a *marchese!* He must wonder at
his luck, at the way they have taken him up."

"He accounts for it by his handsome face, and think
Miss Miller a young lady *qui se passe ses fantaisies!*" said
Mrs. Costello.

"It is very true," Winterbourne pursued, "that Dais
and her mamma have not yet risen to that stage of—wha
shall I call it?—of culture, at which the idea of catching
a count or a *marchese* begins. I believe that they are in
tellectually incapable of that conception."

"Ah! but the *avvocato* can't believe it," said Mrs. Cos
tello.

Of the observation excited by Daisy's "intrigue," Win
terbourne gathered that day at St. Peter's sufficient evi
dence. A dozen of the American colonists in Rome came t
talk with Mrs. Costello, who sat on a little portable stoo
at the base of one of the great pilasters. The vesper servic
was going forward in splendid chants and organ-tones in
the adjacent choir, and meanwhile, between Mrs. Costell
and her friends, there was a great deal said about poo
little Miss Miller's going really "too far." Winterbourn
was not pleased with what he heard; but when, coming ou
upon the great steps of the church, he saw Daisy, who ha
emerged before him, get into an open cab with her accom
plice and roll away through the cynical streets of Rome, h
could not deny to himself that she was going very fa
indeed. He felt very sorry for her—not exactly that h
believed that she had completely lost her head, but be
cause it was painful to hear so much that was pretty and

ndefended and natural assigned to a vulgar place among
e categories of disorder. He made an attempt after this
give a hint to Mrs. Miller. He met one day in the Corso
friend, a tourist like himself, who had just come out of
e Doria Palace, where he had been walking through the
eautiful gallery. His friend talked for a moment about
e superb portrait of Innocent X., by Velasquez, which
angs in one of the cabinets of the palace, and then said,
And in the same cabinet, by-the-way, I had the pleasure
f contemplating a picture of a different kind—that pretty
merican girl whom you pointed out to me last week."
n answer to Winterbourne's inquiries, his friend nar-
ted that the pretty American girl—prettier than ever
was seated with a companion in the secluded nook in
hich the great papal portrait was enshrined.

"Who was her companion?" asked Winterbourne.

"A little Italian with a bouquet in his button-hole. The
irl is delightfully pretty; but I thought I understood
om you the other day that she was a young lady *du
eilleur monde.*"

"So she is!" answered Winterbourne; and having as-
ired himself that his informant had seen Daisy and her
ompanion but five minutes before, he jumped into a
ab and went to call on Mrs. Miller. She was at home; but
e apologized to him for receiving him in Daisy's absence.

"She's gone out somewhere with Mr. Giovanelli," said
Irs. Miller. "She's always going round with Mr. Gio-
anelli."

"I have noticed that they are very intimate," Winter-
ourne observed.

"Oh, it seems as if they couldn't live without each
ther!" said Mrs. Miller. "Well, he's a real gentleman,
nyhow. I keep telling Daisy she's engaged!"

"And what does Daisy say?"

"Oh, she says she isn't engaged. But she might as well
e!" this impartial parent resumed; "she goes on as if
e was. But I've made Mr. Giovanelli promise to tell me,
: *she* doesn't. I should want to write to Mr. Miller about

it—shouldn't you?"

Winterbourne replied that he certainly should; and th
state of mind of Daisy's mamma struck him as so unprec
dented in the annals of parental vigilance that he gav
up as utterly irrelevant the attempt to place her upon he
guard.

After this Daisy was never at home, and Winterbourn
ceased to meet her at the house of their common acquain
ances, because, as he perceived, these shrewd people ha
quite made up their minds that she was going too fa
They ceased to invite her; and they intimated that the
desired to express to observant Europeans the great trut
that, though Miss Daisy Miller was a young America
lady, her behavior was not representative—was regarde
by her compatriots as abnormal. Winterbourne wondere
how she felt about all the cold shoulders that were turne
towards her, and sometimes it annoyed him to suspec
that she did not feel at all. He said to himself that she wa
too light and childish, too uncultivated and unreasonin
too provincial, to have reflected upon her ostracism, o
even to have perceived it. Then at other moments he be
lieved that she carried about in her elegant and irrespo
sible little organism a defiant, passionate, perfectly ob
servant consciousness of the impression she produced. H
asked himself whether Daisy's defiance came from th
consciousness of innocence, or from her being, es
sentially, a young person of the reckless class. It must b
admitted that holding one's self to a belief in Daisy'
"innocence" came to seem to Winterbourne more an
more a matter of fine-spun gallantry. As I have already ha
occasion to relate, he was angry at finding himself reduce
to chopping logic about this young lady; he was vexed a
his want of instinctive certitude as to how far her eccen
tricities were generic, national, and how far they were pe
sonal. From either view of them he had somehow misse
her, and now it was too late. She was "carried away" b
Mr. Giovanelli.

A few days after his brief interview with her mother, h

encountered her in that beautiful abode of flowering desolation known as the Palace of the Cæsars. The early Roman spring had filled the air with bloom and perfume, and the rugged surface of the Palatine was muffled with tender verdure. Daisy was strolling along the top of one of those great mounds of ruin that are embanked with mossy marble and paved with monumental inscriptions. It seemed to him that Rome had never been so lovely as just then. He stood looking off at the enchanting harmony of line and color that remotely encircles the city, inhaling the softly humid odors, and feeling the freshness of the year and the antiquity of the place reaffirm themselves in mysterious interfusion. It seemed to him, also, that Daisy had never looked so pretty; but this had been an observation of his whenever he met her. Giovanelli was at her side, and Giovanelli, too, wore an aspect of even unwonted brilliancy.

"Well," said Daisy, "I should think you would be lonesome!"

"Lonesome?" asked Winterbourne.

"You are always going round by yourself. Can't you get any one to walk with you?"

"I am not so fortunate," said Winterbourne, "as your companion."

Giovanelli, from the first, had treated Winterbourne with distinguished politeness. He listened with a deferential air to his remarks; he laughed punctiliously at his pleasantries; he seemed disposed to testify to his belief that Winterbourne was a superior young man. He carried himself in no degree like a jealous wooer; he had obviously a great deal of tact; he had no objection to your expecting a little humility of him. It even seemed to Winterbourne at times that Giovanelli would find a certain mental relief in being able to have a private understanding with him—to say to him, as an intelligent man, that, bless you, *he* knew how extraordinary was this young lady, and didn't flatter himself with delusive—or, at least, *too* delusive—hopes of matrimony and dollars. On this occasion he strolled away from his companion to pluck a sprig of almond-blossom, which he carefully arranged in his buttonhole.

"I know why you say that," said Daisy, watching Giovanelli. "Because you think I go round too much with *him*." And she nodded at her attendant.

"Every one thinks so—if you care to know," said Winterbourne.

"Of course I care to know!" Daisy exclaimed, seriously. "But I don't believe it. They are only pretending to be shocked. They don't really care a straw what I do. Besides, I don't go round so much."

"I think you will find they do care. They will show it disagreeably."

Daisy looked at him a moment. "How disagreeably?"

"Haven't you noticed anything?" Winterbourne asked.

"I have noticed you. But I noticed you were as stiff as an umbrella the first time I saw you."

"You will find I am not so stiff as several others," said Winterbourne, smiling.

"How shall I find it?"

"By going to see the others."

"What will they do to me?"

"They will give you the cold shoulder. Do you know what that means?"

Daisy was looking at him intently; she began to color. "Do you mean as Mrs. Walker did the other night?"

"Exactly!" said Winterbourne.

She looked away at Giovanelli, who was decorating himself with his almond-blossom. Then, looking back at Winterbourne, "I shouldn't think you would let people be so unkind!" she said.

"How can I help it?" he asked.

"I should think you would say something."

"I did say something;" and he paused a moment. "I say that your mother tells me that she believes you are engaged."

"Well, she does," said Daisy, very simply.

Winterbourne began to laugh. "And does Randolph
lieve it?" he asked.

"I guess Randolph doesn't believe anything," said
isy. Randolph's scepticism excited Winterbourne to
rther hilarity, and he observed that Giovanelli was com-
g back to them. Daisy, observing it too, addressed herself
ain to her countryman. "Since you have mentioned it,"
e said, "I *am* engaged." . . . Winterbourne looked at
r; he had stopped laughing. "You don't believe it!" she
ded.

He was silent a moment; and then, "Yes, I believe it,"
said.

"Oh, no, you don't!" she answered. "Well, then—I am
t!"

The young girl and her cicerone were on their way to
e gate of the enclosure, so that Winterbourne, who had
t lately entered, presently took leave of them. A week
terwards he went to dine at a beautiful villa on the
elian Hill, and, on arriving, dismissed his hired vehicle.
e evening was charming, and he promised himself the
tisfaction of walking home beneath the Arch of Con-
ntine and past the vaguely-lighted monuments of the
rum. There was a waning moon in the sky, and her
diance was not brilliant, but she was veiled in a thin
ud-curtain which seemed to diffuse and equalize it.
hen, on his return from the villa (it was eleven o'clock),
interbourne approached the dusky circle of the Colos-
um, it occurred to him, as a lover of the picturesque,
at the interior, in the pale moonshine, would be well
rth a glance. He turned aside and walked to one of the
pty arches, near which, as he observed, an open carriage
ne of the little Roman street-cabs—was stationed. Then
passed in, among the cavernous shadows of the great
ucture, and emerged upon the clear and silent arena.
e place had never seemed to him more impressive. One-
lf of the gigantic circus was in deep shade, the other was
eping in the luminous dusk. As he stood there he began
murmur Byron's famous lines, out of "Manfred"; but

before he had finished his quotation he remembered th:
if nocturnal meditations in the Colosseum are recor
mended by the poets, they are deprecated by the docto:
The historic atmosphere was there, certainly; but tl
historic atmosphere, scientifically considered, was no be
ter than a villainous miasma. Winterbourne walked to tl
middle of the arena, to take a more general glance, i:
tending thereafter to make a hasty retreat. The gre:
cross in the centre was covered with shadow; it was only
he drew near it that he made it out distinctly. Then he sa
that two persons were stationed upon the low steps whic
formed its base. One of these was a woman, seated; h:
companion was standing in front of her.

Presently the sound of the woman's voice came to hi:
distinctly in the warm night air: "Well, he looks at
as one of the old lions or tigers may have looked at tl
Christian martyrs!" These were the words he heard in tl
familiar accent of Miss Daisy Miller.

"Let us hope he is not very hungry," responded th
ingenious Giovanelli. "He will have to take me first; yo
will serve for dessert!"

Winterbourne stopped, with a sort of horror, and,
must be added, with a sort of relief. It was as if a sudde
illumination had been flashed upon the ambiguity
Daisy's behavior, and the riddle had become easy to rea
She was a young lady whom a gentleman need no long:
be at pains to respect. He stood there looking at her
looking at her companion, and not reflecting that thoug
he saw them vaguely, he himself must have been mo:
brightly visible. He felt angry with himself that he ha
bothered so much about the right way of regarding Mi
Daisy Miller. Then, as he was going to advance again, b
checked himself; not from the fear that he was doing he
injustice, but from the sense of the danger of appearin
unbecomingly exhilarated by this sudden revulsion fro:
cautious criticism. He turned away towards the entranc
of the place, but, as he did so, he heard Daisy speak agai:

"Why, it was Mr. Winterbourne! He saw me, and h

uts me!"

What a clever little reprobate she was, and how smartly he played at injured innocence! But he wouldn't cut her. Winterbourne came forward again, and went towards he great cross. Daisy had got up; Giovanelli lifted his hat. Winterbourne had now begun to think simply of the craziness, from a sanitary point of view, of a delicate young irl lounging away the evening in this nest of malaria. What if she *were* a clever little reprobate? that was no eason for her dying of the *perniciosa*. "How long have ou been here?" he asked, almost brutally.

Daisy, lovely in the flattering moonlight, looked at him moment. Then—"All the evening," she answered, gently. . . "I never saw anything so pretty."

"I am afraid," said Winterbourne, "that you will not hink Roman fever very pretty. This is the way people atch it. I wonder," he added, turning to Giovanelli, "that ou, a native Roman, should countenance such a terrible ndiscretion."

"Ah," said the handsome native, "for myself I am not fraid."

"Neither am I—for you! I am speaking for this young ady."

Giovanelli lifted his well-shaped eyebrows and showed is brilliant teeth. But he took Winterbourne's rebuke vith docility. "I told the signorina it was a grave indis-retion; but when was the signorina ever prudent?"

"I never was sick, and I don't mean to be!" the sig-norina declared. " I don't look like much, but I'm healthy! was bound to see the Colosseum by moonlight; I houldn't have wanted to go home without that; and we iave had the most beautiful time, haven't we, Mr. Gio-anelli? If there has been any danger, Eugenio can give ne some pills. He has got some splendid pills."

"I should advise you," said Winterbourne, "to drive iome as fast as possible and take one!"

"What you say is very wise," Giovanelli rejoined. "I vill go and make sure the carriage is at hand." And he went forward rapidly.

Daisy followed with Winterbourne. He kept looking at her; she seemed not in the least embarrassed. Winterbourne said nothing; Daisy chattered about the beauty of the place. "Well, I *have* seen the Colosseum by moonlight!" she exclaimed. "That's one good thing." Then noticing Winterbourne's silence, she asked him why he didn't speak. He made no answer; he only began to laugh. They passed under one of the dark archways; Giovanelli was in front with the carriage. Here Daisy stopped a moment, looking at the young American. "*Did* you believe I was engaged the other day?" she asked.

"It doesn't matter what I believed the other day," said Winterbourne, still laughing.

"Well, what do you believe now?"

"I believe that it makes very little difference whether you are engaged or not!"

He felt the young girl's pretty eyes fixed upon him through the thick gloom of the archway; she was apparently going to answer. But Giovanelli hurried her forward. "Quick! quick!" he said; "if we get in by midnight we are quite safe."

Daisy took her seat in the carriage, and the fortunate Italian placed himself beside her. "Don't forget Eugenio's pills!" said Winterbourne, as he lifted his hat.

"I don't care," said Daisy, in a little strange tone, "whether I have Roman fever or not!" Upon this the cab driver cracked his whip, and they rolled away over the desultory patches of the antique pavement.

Winterbourne, to do him justice, as it were, mentioned to no one that he had encountered Miss Miller, at midnight, in the Colosseum with a gentleman; but, nevertheless, a couple of days later, the fact of her having been there under these circumstances was known to every member of the little American circle, and commented accordingly. Winterbourne reflected that they had of course known it at the hotel, and, that, after Daisy's return there had been an exchange of remarks between the porter and

e cab-driver. But the young man was conscious, at the
me moment, that it had ceased to be a matter of serious
gret to him that the little American flirt should be
alked about" by low-minded menials. These people, a
y or two later, had serious information to give: the little
merican flirt was alarmingly ill. Winterbourne, when
e rumor came to him, immediately went to the hotel
r more news. He found that two or three charitable
iends had preceded him, and that they were being en-
rtained in Mrs. Miller's salon by Randolph.

"It's going round at night," said Randolph—"that's
hat made her sick. She's always going round at night.
shouldn't think she'd want to, it's so plaguy dark. You
n't see anything here at night, except when there's a
oon! In America there's always a moon!" Mrs. Miller
as invisible; she was now, at least, giving her daughter
e advantage of her society. It was evident that Daisy was
angerously ill.

Winterbourne went often to ask for news of her, and
nce he saw Mrs. Miller, who, though deeply alarmed,
as, rather to his surprise, perfectly composed, and, as
appeared, a most efficient and judicious nurse. She talked
good deal about Dr. Davis, but Winterbourne paid her
e compliment of saying to himself that she was not,
ter all, such a monstrous goose. "Daisy spoke of you the
her day," she said to him. "Half the time she doesn't
now what she's saying, but that time I think she did. She
ave me a message. She told me to tell you—she told me to
ll you that she never was engaged to that handsome
alian. I am sure I am very glad. Mr. Giovanelli hasn't
een near us since she was taken ill. I thought he was so
uch of a gentleman; but I don't call that very polite! A
dy told me that he was afraid I was angry with him for
king Daisy round at night. Well, so I am; but I suppose
e knows I'm a lady. I would scorn to scold him. Anyway,
e says she's not engaged. I don't know why she wanted
ou to know; but she said to me three times, 'Mind you
ll Mr. Winterbourne.' And then she told me to ask if

you remembered the time you went to that castle in Switzerland. But I said I wouldn't give any such messages as that. Only, if she is not engaged, I'm sure I'm glad to know it."

But, as Winterbourne had said, it mattered very little. A week after this the poor girl died; it had been a terrible case of the fever. Daisy's grave was in the little Protestant cemetery, in an angle of the wall of imperial Rome, beneath the cypresses and the thick spring-flowers. Winterbourne stood there beside it, with a number of other mourners—a number larger than the scandal excited by the young lady's career would have led you to expect. Near him stood Giovanelli, who came nearer still before Winterbourne turned away. Giovanelli was very pale: on this occasion he had no flower in his button-hole; he seemed to wish to say something. At last he said, "She was the most beautiful young lady I ever saw, and the most amiable"; and then he added in a moment, "and she was the most innocent."

Winterbourne looked at him, and presently repeated his words, "And the most innocent?"

"The most innocent!"

Winterbourne felt sore and angry. "Why, the devil," he asked, "did you take her to that fatal place?"

Mr. Giovanelli's urbanity was apparently imperturbable. He looked on the ground a moment, and then he said, "For myself I had no fear; and she wanted to go."

"That was no reason!" Winterbourne declared.

The subtle Roman again dropped his eyes. "If she had lived, I should have got nothing. She would never have married me, I am sure."

"She would never have married you?"

"For a moment I hoped so. But no. I am sure."

Winterbourne listened to him: he stood staring at the raw protuberance among the April daisies. When he turned away again, Mr. Giovanelli with his light, slow step, had retired.

Winterbourne almost immediately left Rome; but the

ollowing summer he again met his aunt, Mrs. Costello, t Vevay. Mrs. Costello was fond of Vevay. In the interval Winterbourne had often thought of Daisy Miller and her mystifying manners. One day he spoke of her to his aunt— aid it was on his conscience that he had done her in- ustice.

"I am sure I don't know," said Mrs. Costello. "How did our injustice affect her?"

"She sent me a message before her death which I didn't nderstand at the time; but I have understood it since. he would have appreciated one's esteem."

"Is that a modest way," asked Mrs. Costello, "of saying hat she would have reciprocated one's affection?"

Winterbourne offered no answer to this question; but e presently said, "You were right in that remark that ou made last summer. I was booked to make a mistake. I ave lived too long in foreign parts."

Nevertheless, he went back to live at Geneva, whence here continue to come the most contradictory accounts f his motives of sojourn: a report that he is "studying" ard—an intimation that he is much interested in a very lever foreign lady.

THE LAUREL THOMAS HARDY

JUDE THE OBSCURE 75

The novel that shocked the Victorian world with its frank perceptive treatment of human instincts and passions.

TESS OF THE D'URBERVILLES 60

This poignant tragedy of a betrayed woman is the most famous and probably the best of Hardy's novels.

RETURN OF THE NATIVE 60

Somber Egdon Heath is the backdrop for this moody masterpiece, introducing the most colorful heroine in Hardy's fiction.

THE MAYOR OF CASTERBRIDGE 50

Egotism and obstinacy bring about the ruin of a domineering tradesman.

If you cannot obtain copies of these titles at your local newsstand, just send the price (plus 10c per copy for handling and postage) to Dell Books, Box 2291, Grand Central Post Office, New York 17, N.Y. No postage or handling charge is required on any order of five or more books.